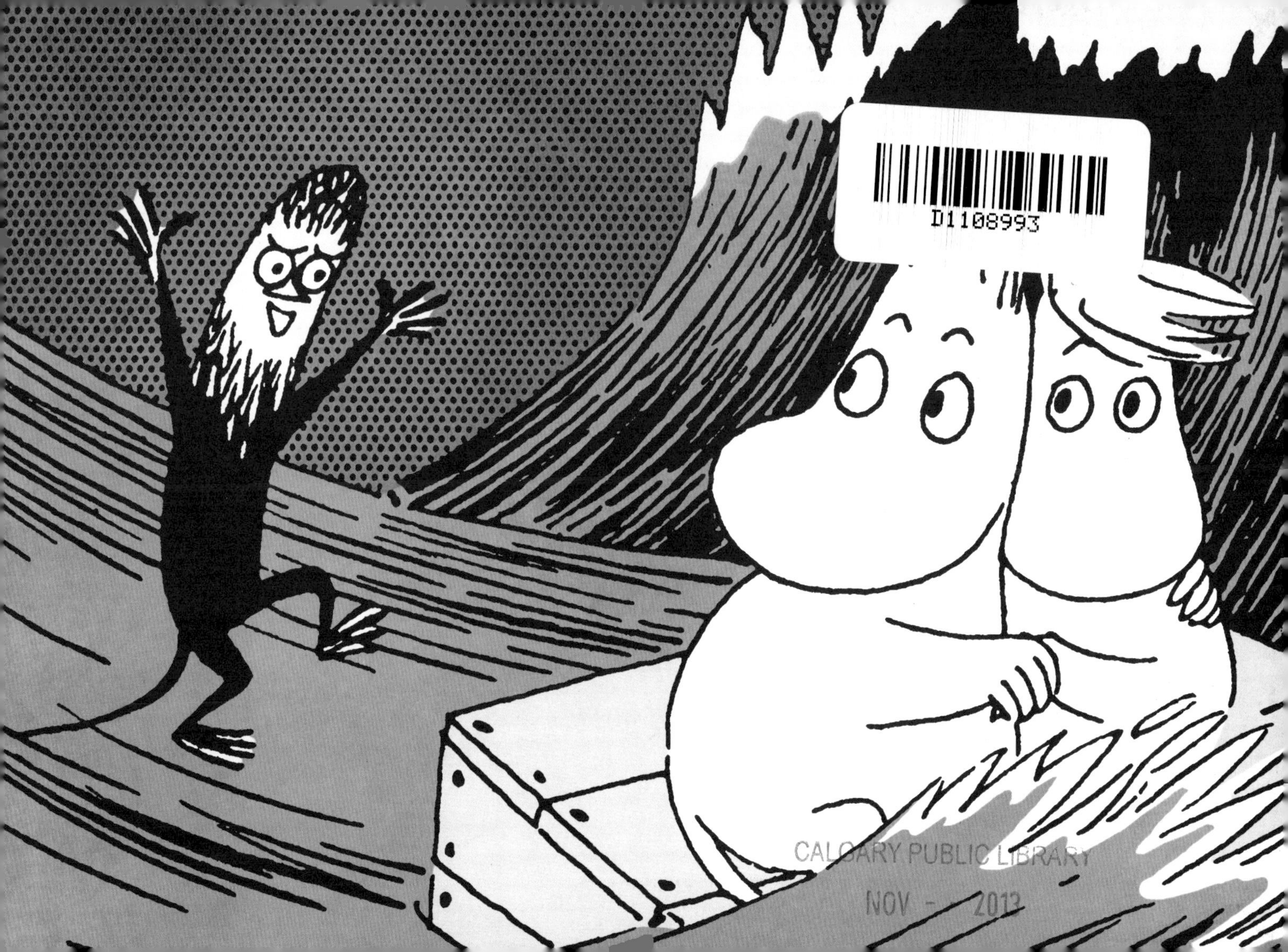

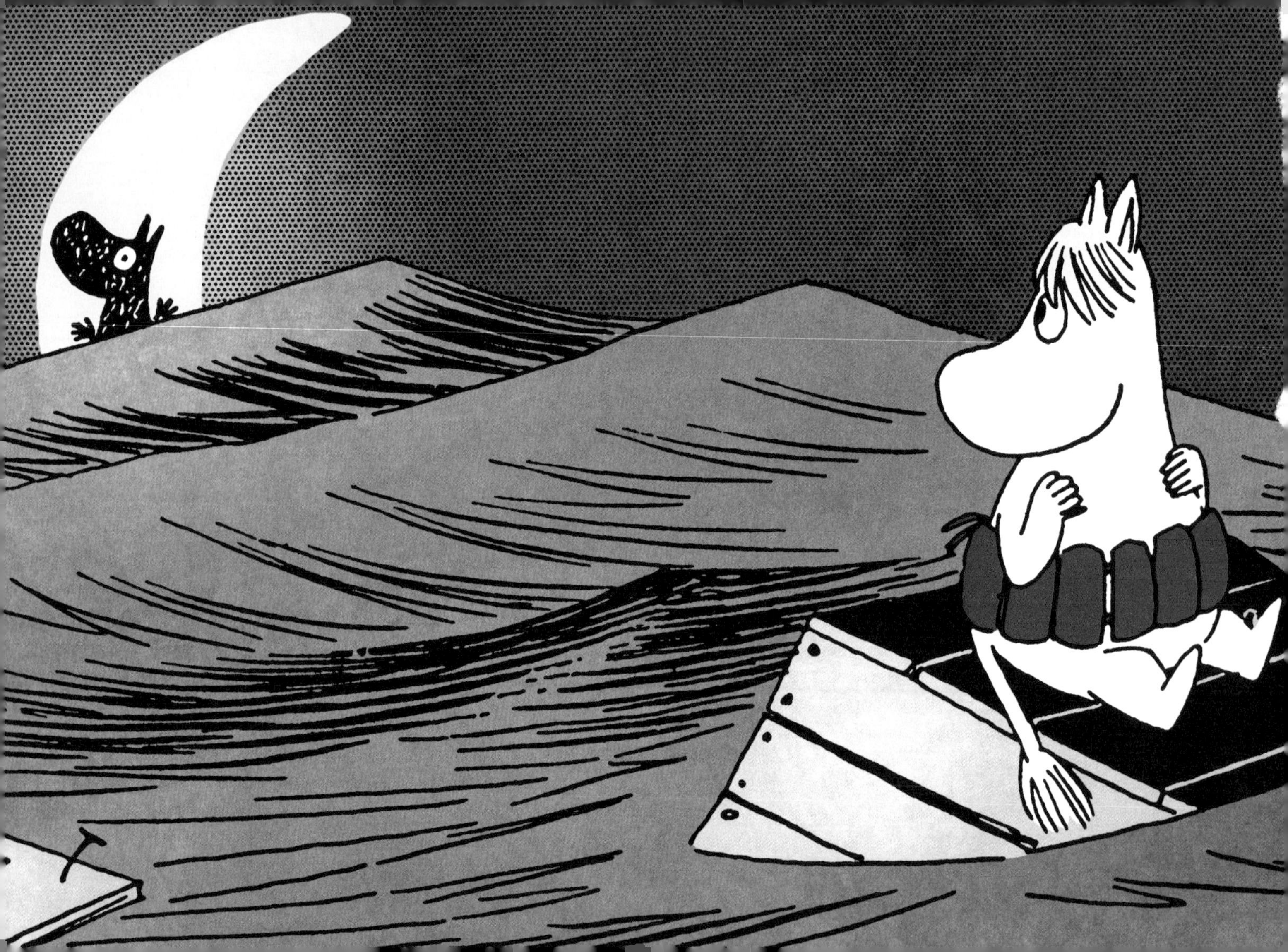

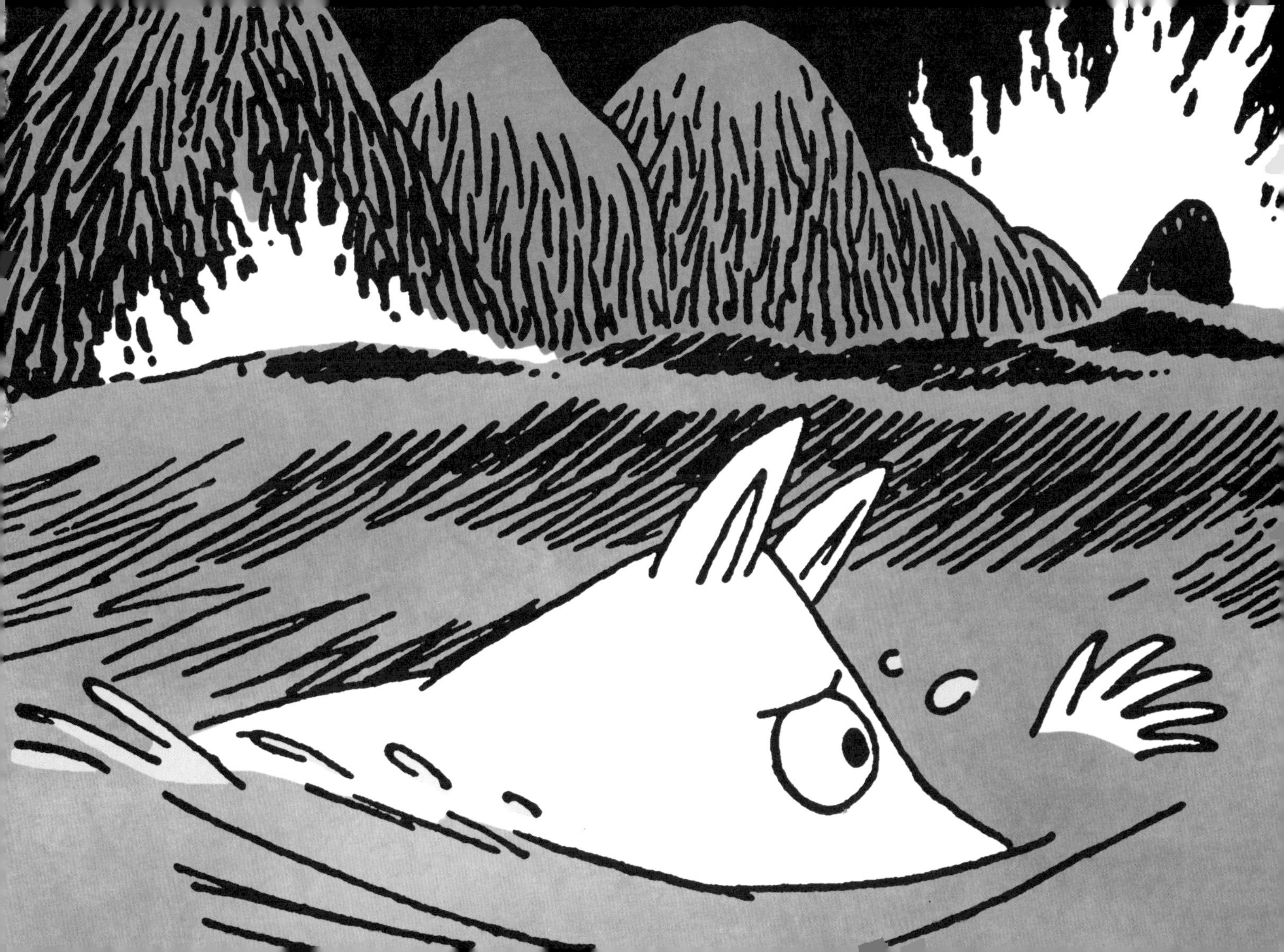

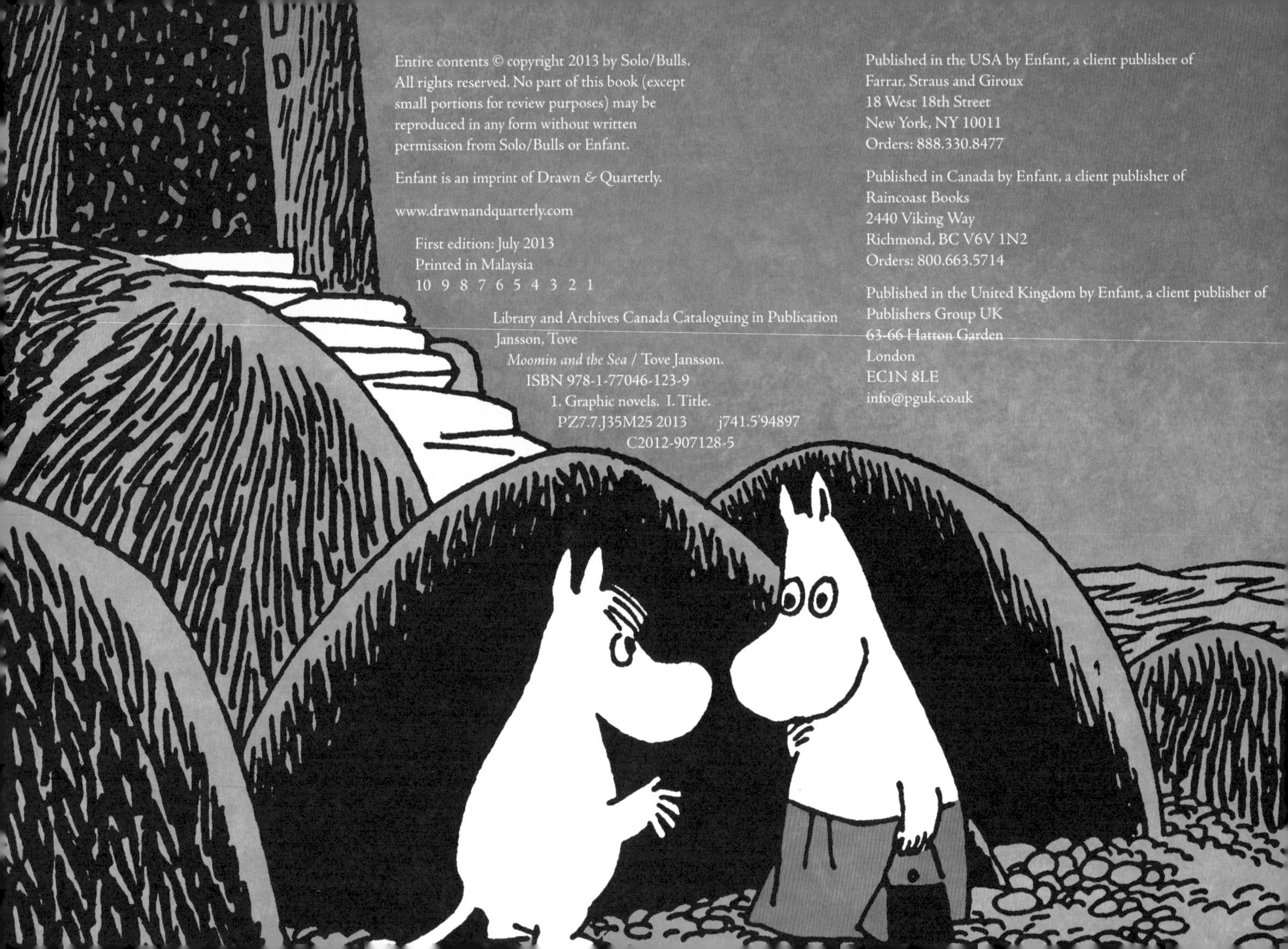

Enfant is an imprint of Drawn & Quarterly.

www.drawnandquarterly.com

First edition: July 2013
Printed in Malaysia
10 9 8 7 6 5 4 3 2 1

Library and Archives Canada Cataloguing in Publication
Jansson, Tove
Moomin and the Sea / Tove Jansson.
ISBN 978-1-77046-123-9
1. Graphic novels. I. Title.
PZ7.7.J35M25 2013 j741.5'94897
C2012-907128-5

Published in the USA by Enfant, a client publisher of
Farrar, Straus and Giroux
18 West 18th Street
New York, NY 10011
Orders: 888.330.8477

Published in Canada by Enfant, a client publisher of
Raincoast Books
2440 Viking Way
Richmond, BC V6V 1N2
Orders: 800.663.5714

Published in the United Kingdom by Enfant, a client publisher of
Publishers Group UK
63-66 Hatton Garden
London
EC1N 8LE
info@pguk.co.uk

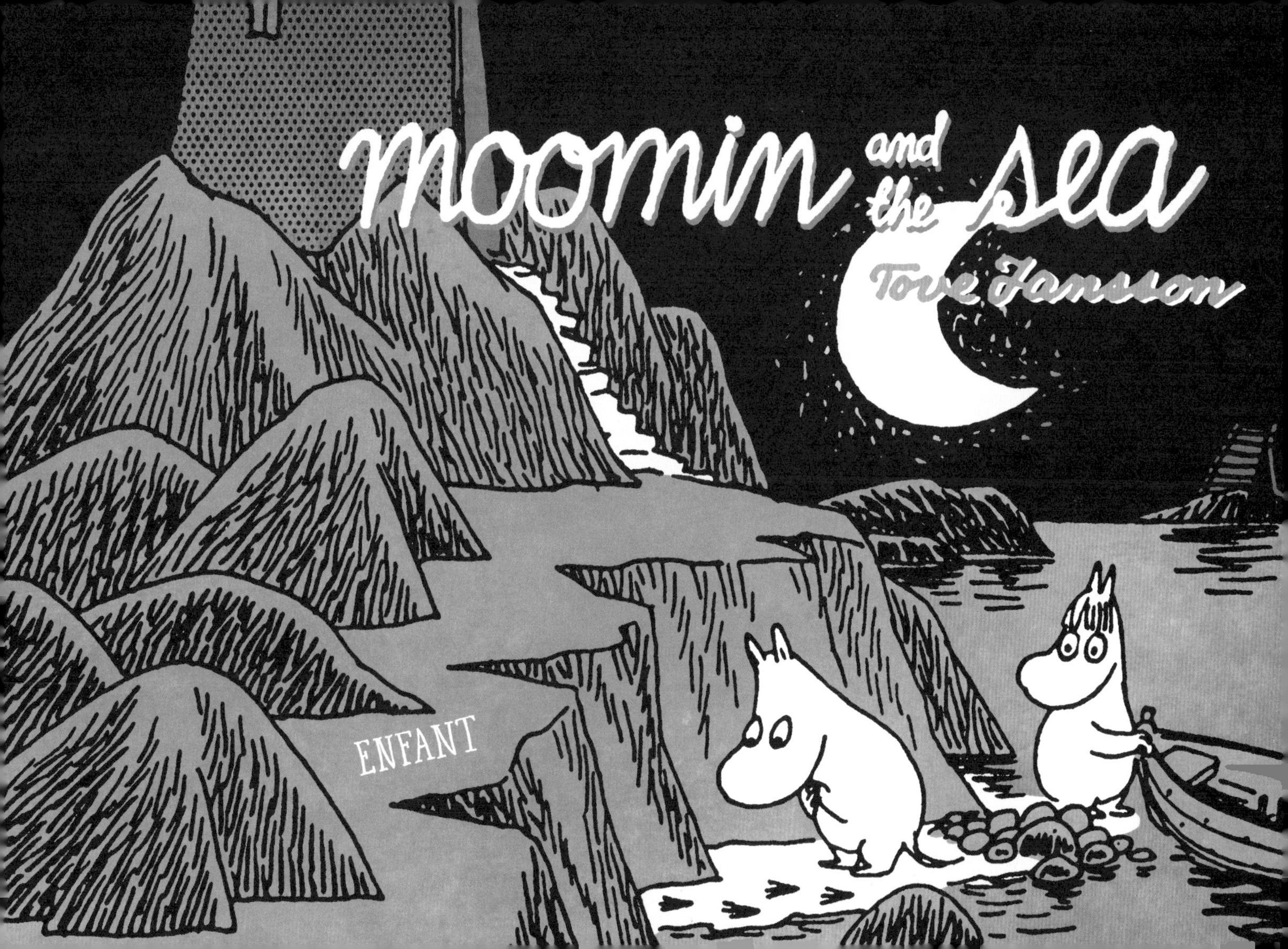
moomin and the sea
Tove Jansson
ENFANT

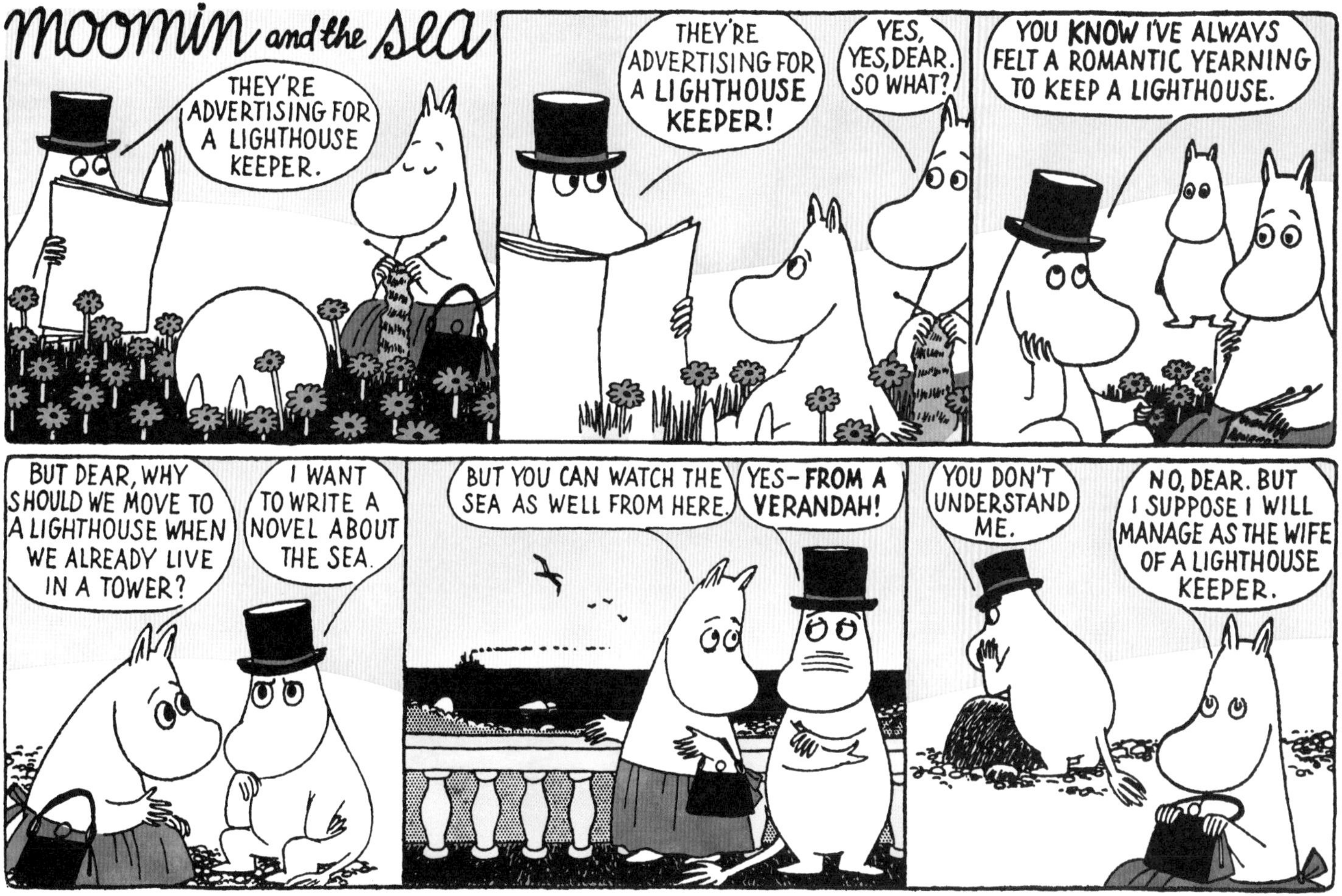
moomin and the sea
THEY'RE ADVERTISING FOR A LIGHTHOUSE KEEPER.
THEY'RE ADVERTISING FOR A LIGHTHOUSE KEEPER!
YES, YES, DEAR. SO WHAT?
YOU KNOW I'VE ALWAYS FELT A ROMANTIC YEARNING TO KEEP A LIGHTHOUSE.
BUT DEAR, WHY SHOULD WE MOVE TO A LIGHTHOUSE WHEN WE ALREADY LIVE IN A TOWER?
I WANT TO WRITE A NOVEL ABOUT THE SEA.
BUT YOU CAN WATCH THE SEA AS WELL FROM HERE.
YES- FROM A VERANDAH!
YOU DON'T UNDERSTAND ME.
NO, DEAR. BUT I SUPPOSE I WILL MANAGE AS THE WIFE OF A LIGHTHOUSE KEEPER.

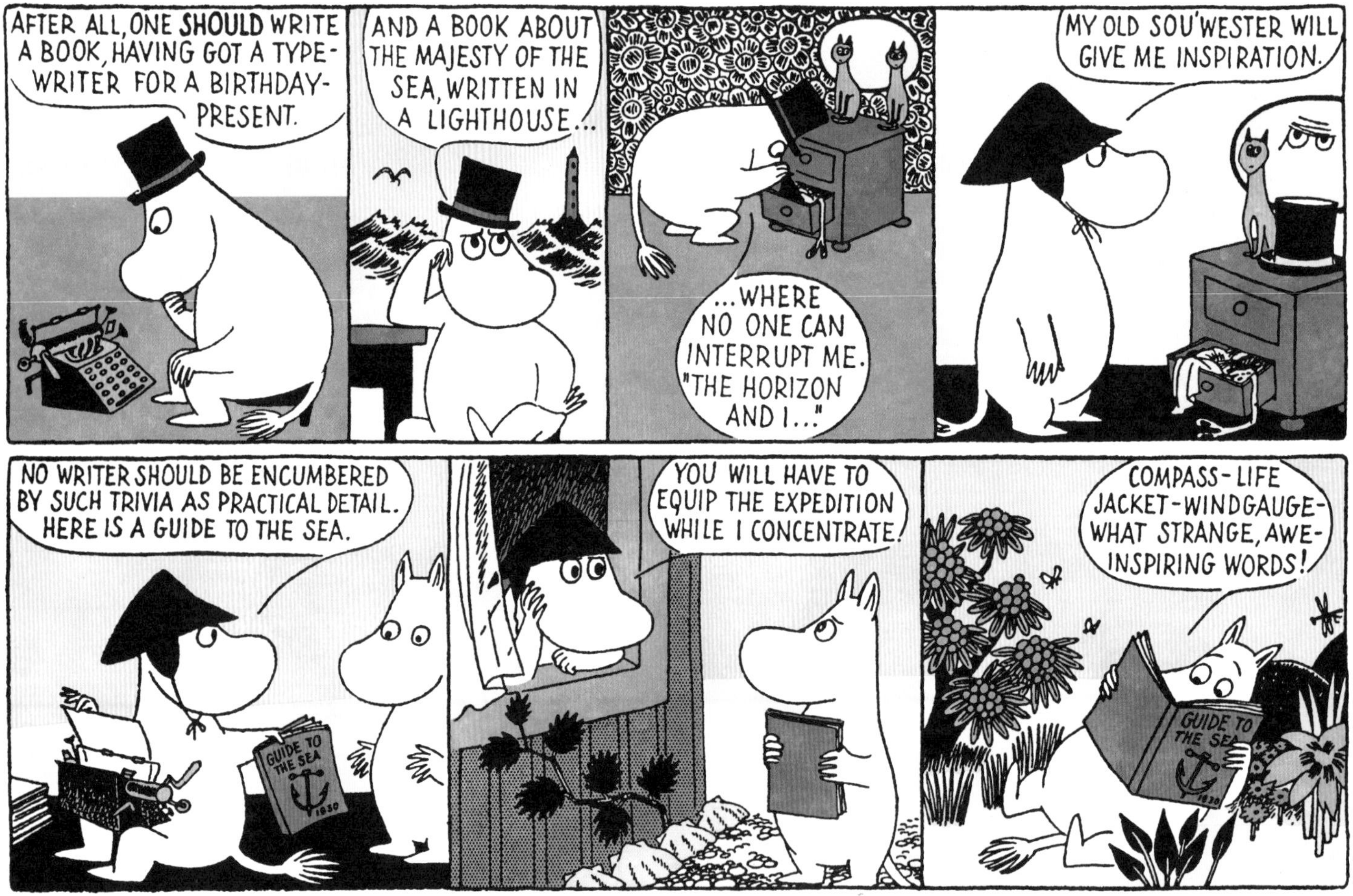
AFTER ALL, ONE SHOULD WRITE A BOOK, HAVING GOT A TYPE-WRITER FOR A BIRTHDAY-PRESENT.
AND A BOOK ABOUT THE MAJESTY OF THE SEA, WRITTEN IN A LIGHTHOUSE...
...WHERE NO ONE CAN INTERRUPT ME. "THE HORIZON AND I..."
MY OLD SOU'WESTER WILL GIVE ME INSPIRATION.
NO WRITER SHOULD BE ENCUMBERED BY SUCH TRIVIA AS PRACTICAL DETAIL. HERE IS A GUIDE TO THE SEA.
GUIDE TO THE SEA
1930
YOU WILL HAVE TO EQUIP THE EXPEDITION WHILE I CONCENTRATE.
COMPASS-LIFE JACKET-WINDGAUGE-WHAT STRANGE, AWE-INSPIRING WORDS!
GUIDE TO THE SEA
1930

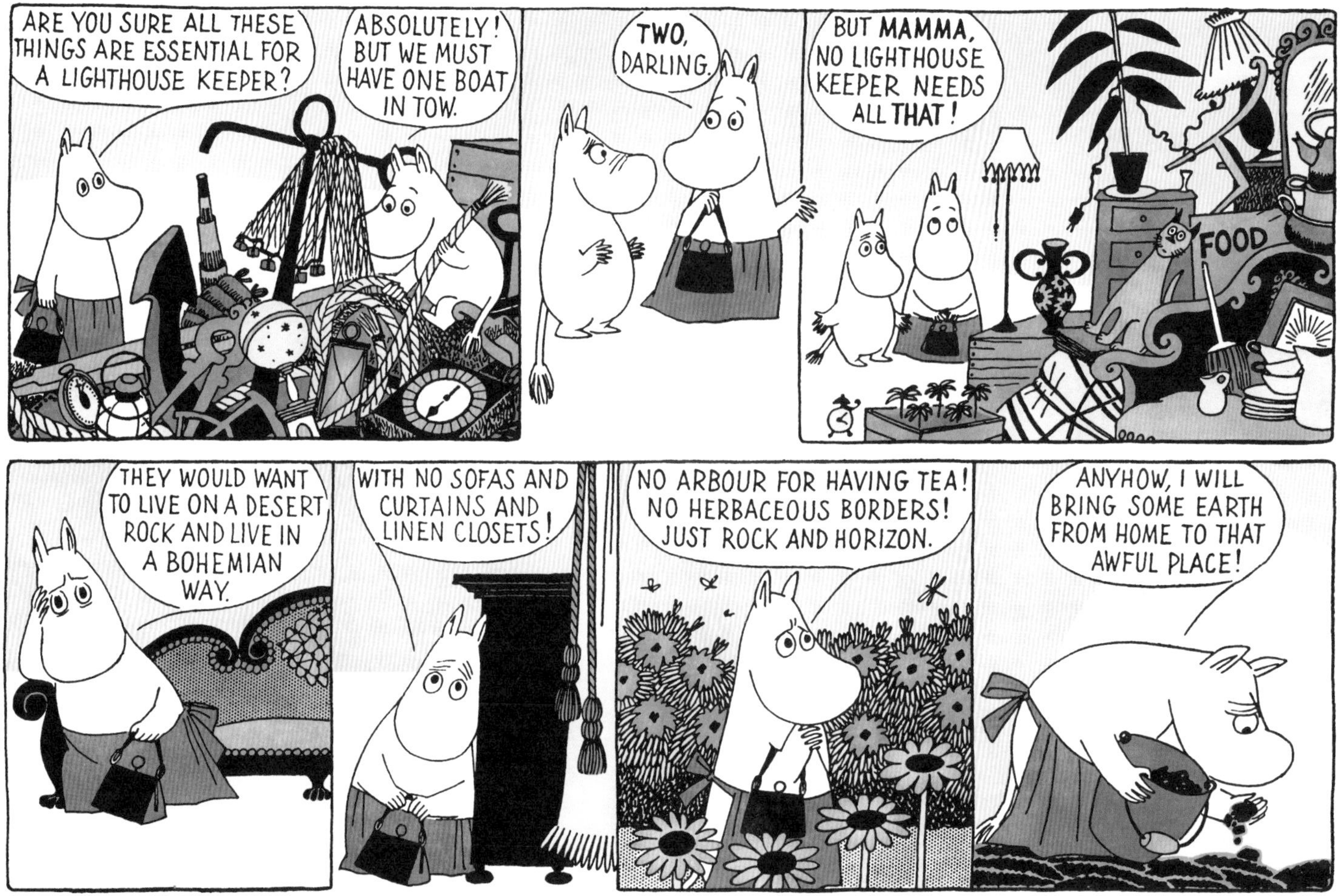
ARE YOU SURE ALL THESE THINGS ARE ESSENTIAL FOR A LIGHTHOUSE KEEPER?
ABSOLUTELY! BUT WE MUST HAVE ONE BOAT IN TOW.
TWO, DARLING.
BUT MAMMA, NO LIGHTHOUSE KEEPER NEEDS ALL THAT!
FOOD
THEY WOULD WANT TO LIVE ON A DESERT ROCK AND LIVE IN A BOHEMIAN WAY.
WITH NO SOFAS AND CURTAINS AND LINEN CLOSETS!
NO ARBOUR FOR HAVING TEA! NO HERBACEOUS BORDERS! JUST ROCK AND HORIZON.
ANYHOW, I WILL BRING SOME EARTH FROM HOME TO THAT AWFUL PLACE!

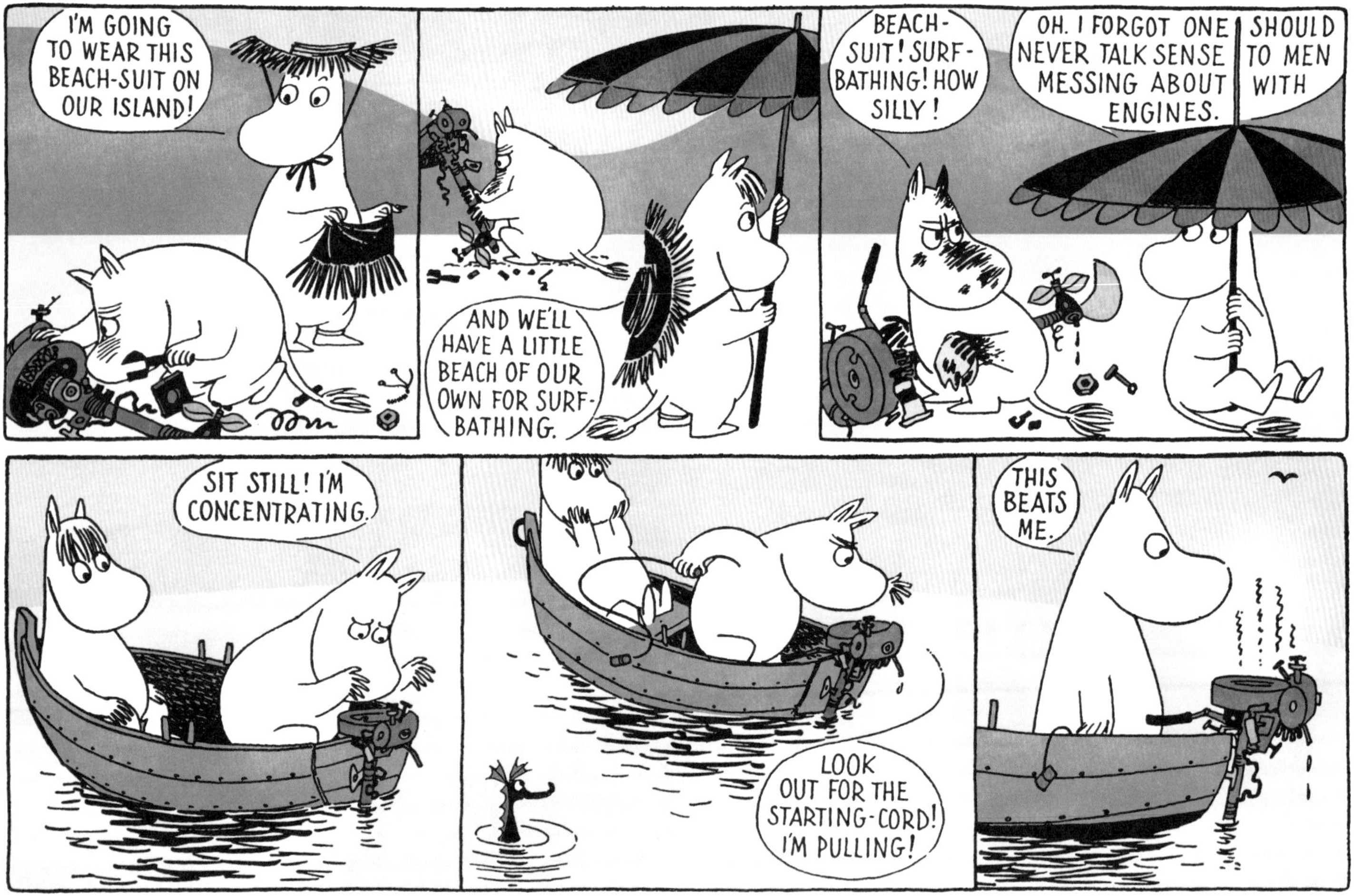
I'M GOING TO WEAR THIS BEACH-SUIT ON OUR ISLAND!
AND WE'LL HAVE A LITTLE BEACH OF OUR OWN FOR SURF-BATHING.
BEACH-SUIT! SURF-BATHING! HOW SILLY!
OH. I FORGOT ONE NEVER TALK SENSE MESSING ABOUT ENGINES.
SHOULD TO MEN WITH
SIT STILL! I'M CONCENTRATING.
LOOK OUT FOR THE STARTING-CORD! I'M PULLING!
THIS BEATS ME.

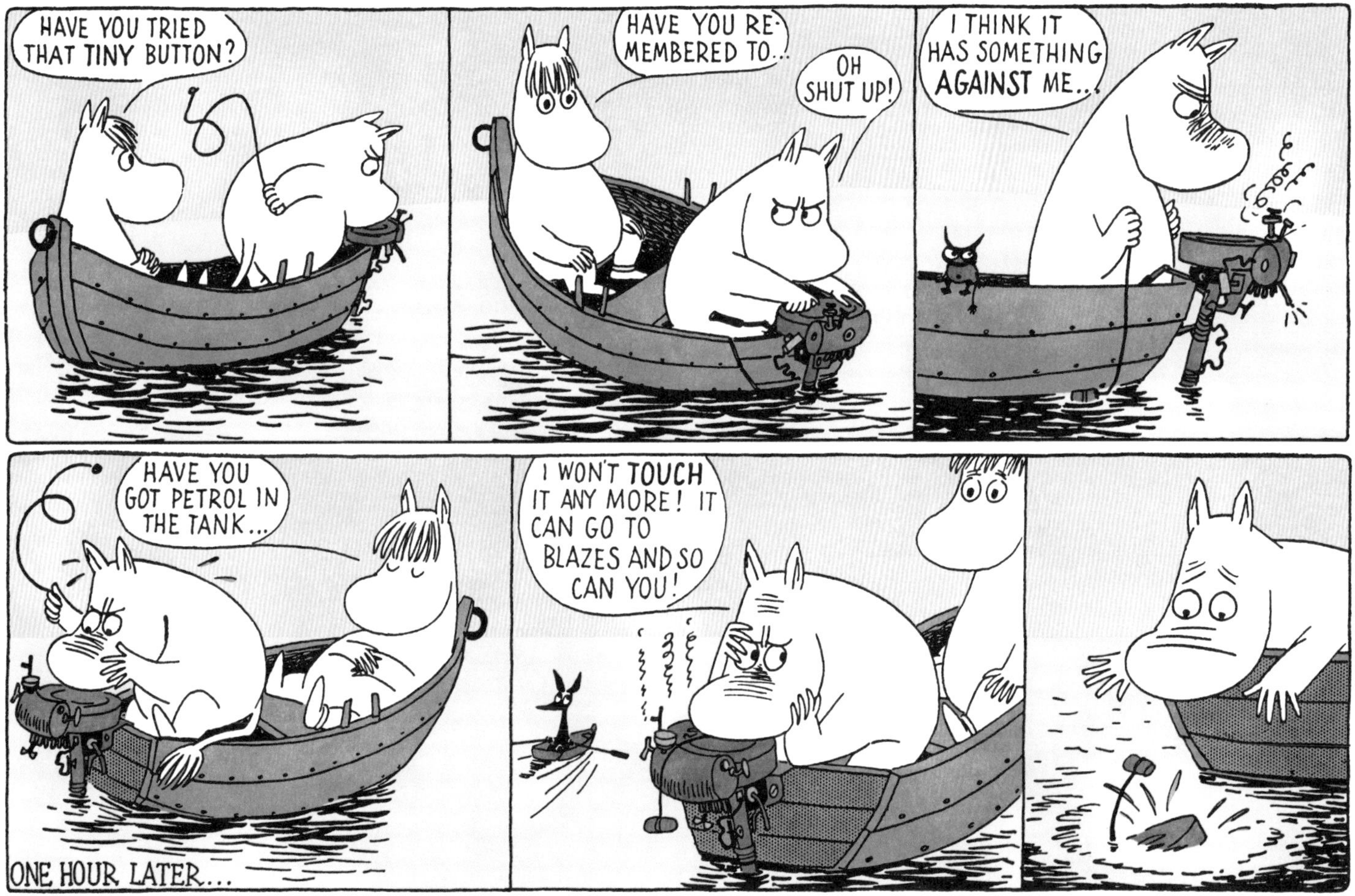
HAVE YOU TRIED THAT TINY BUTTON?
HAVE YOU RE-MEMBERED TO...
OH SHUT UP!
I THINK IT HAS SOMETHING AGAINST ME...
ONE HOUR LATER...
HAVE YOU GOT PETROL IN THE TANK...
I WON'T TOUCH IT ANY MORE! IT CAN GO TO BLAZES AND SO CAN YOU!

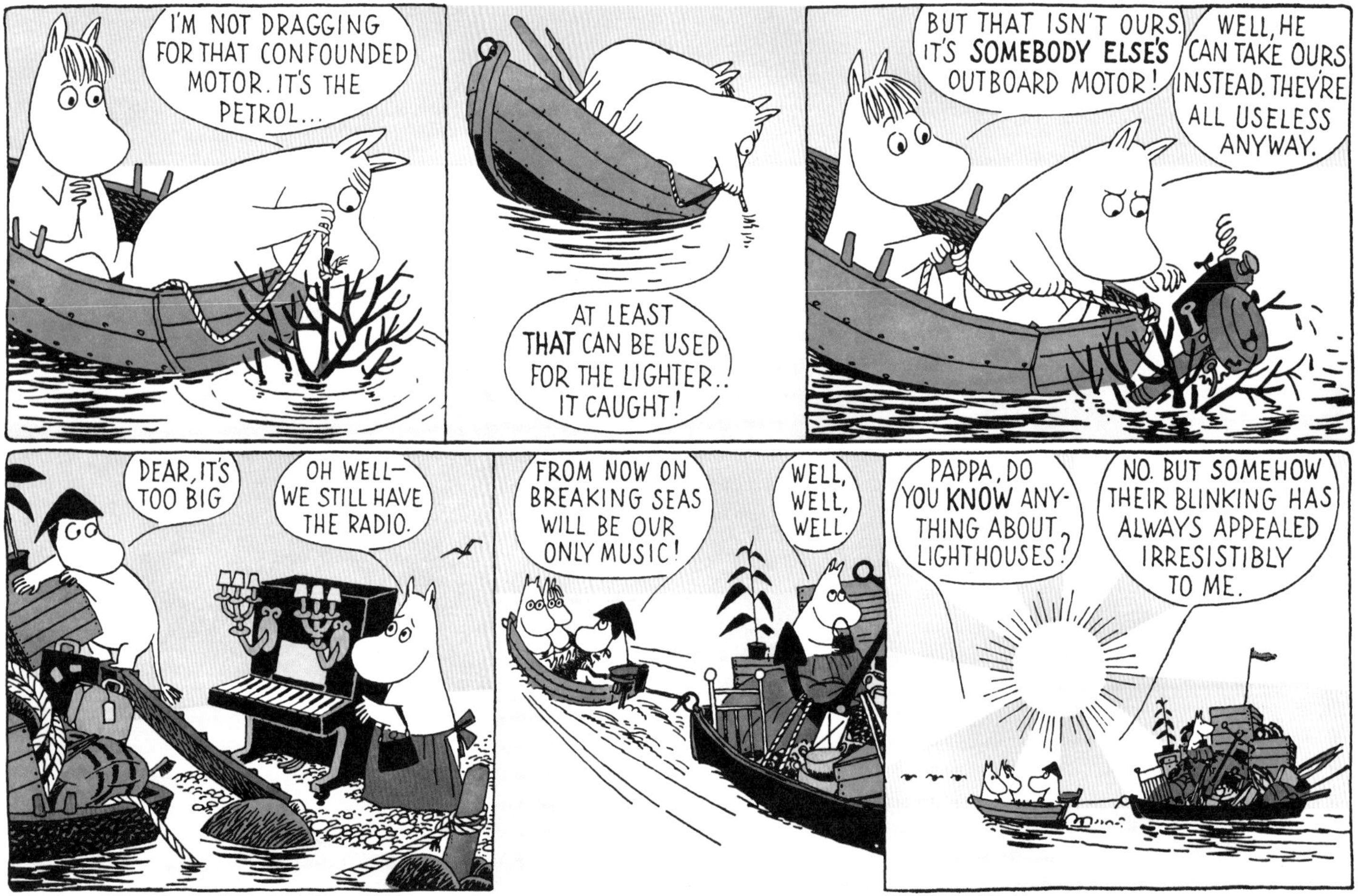
I'M NOT DRAGGING FOR THAT CONFOUNDED MOTOR. IT'S THE PETROL...
AT LEAST THAT CAN BE USED FOR THE LIGHTER.. IT CAUGHT!
BUT THAT ISN'T OURS. IT'S SOMEBODY ELSE'S OUTBOARD MOTOR!
WELL, HE CAN TAKE OURS INSTEAD. THEY'RE ALL USELESS ANYWAY.
DEAR, IT'S TOO BIG
OH WELL— WE STILL HAVE THE RADIO.
FROM NOW ON BREAKING SEAS WILL BE OUR ONLY MUSIC!
WELL, WELL, WELL.
PAPPA, DO YOU KNOW ANY-THING ABOUT LIGHTHOUSES?
NO. BUT SOMEHOW THEIR BLINKING HAS ALWAYS APPEALED IRRESISTIBLY TO ME.

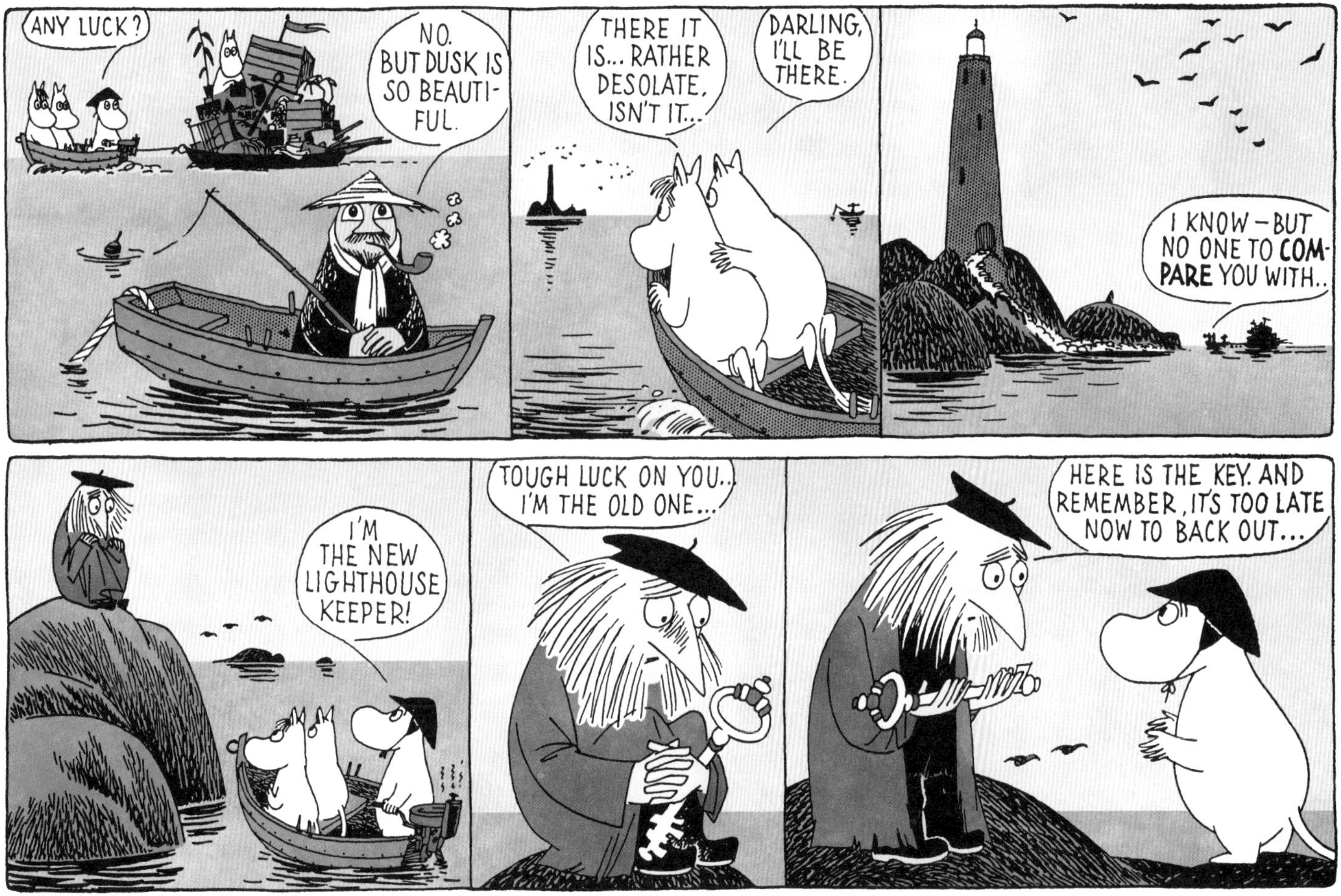
ANY LUCK?
NO. BUT DUSK IS SO BEAUTIFUL.
THERE IT IS... RATHER DESOLATE, ISN'T IT...
DARLING, I'LL BE THERE.
I KNOW—BUT NO ONE TO **COMPARE** YOU WITH..
I'M THE NEW LIGHTHOUSE KEEPER!
TOUGH LUCK ON YOU.. I'M THE OLD ONE...
HERE IS THE KEY. AND REMEMBER, IT'S TOO LATE NOW TO BACK OUT...

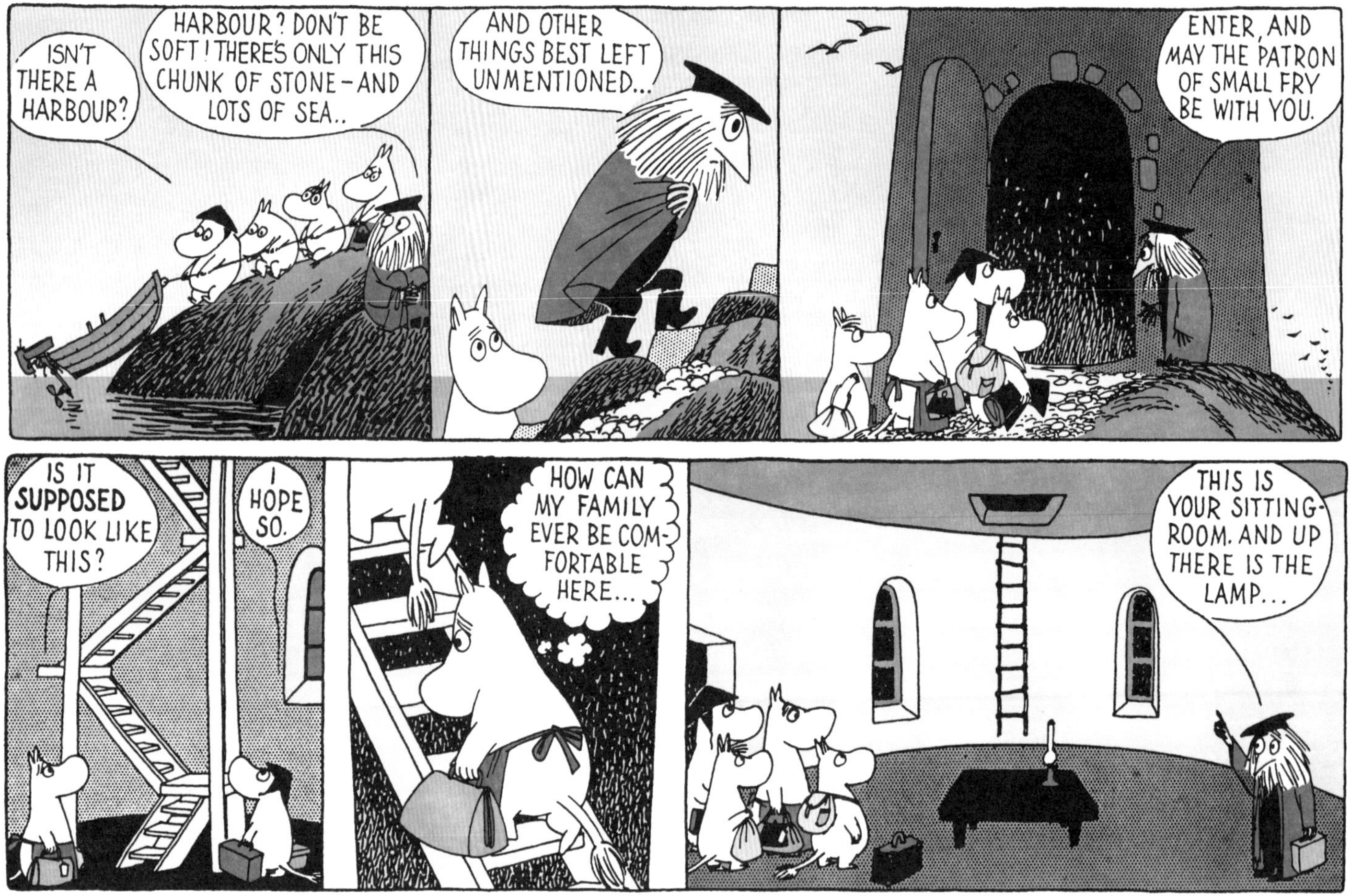
ISN'T THERE A HARBOUR?
HARBOUR? DON'T BE SOFT! THERE'S ONLY THIS CHUNK OF STONE - AND LOTS OF SEA..
AND OTHER THINGS BEST LEFT UNMENTIONED...
ENTER, AND MAY THE PATRON OF SMALL FRY BE WITH YOU.
IS IT **SUPPOSED** TO LOOK LIKE THIS?
I HOPE SO.
HOW CAN MY FAMILY EVER BE COMFORTABLE HERE...
THIS IS YOUR SITTING-ROOM. AND UP THERE IS THE LAMP...

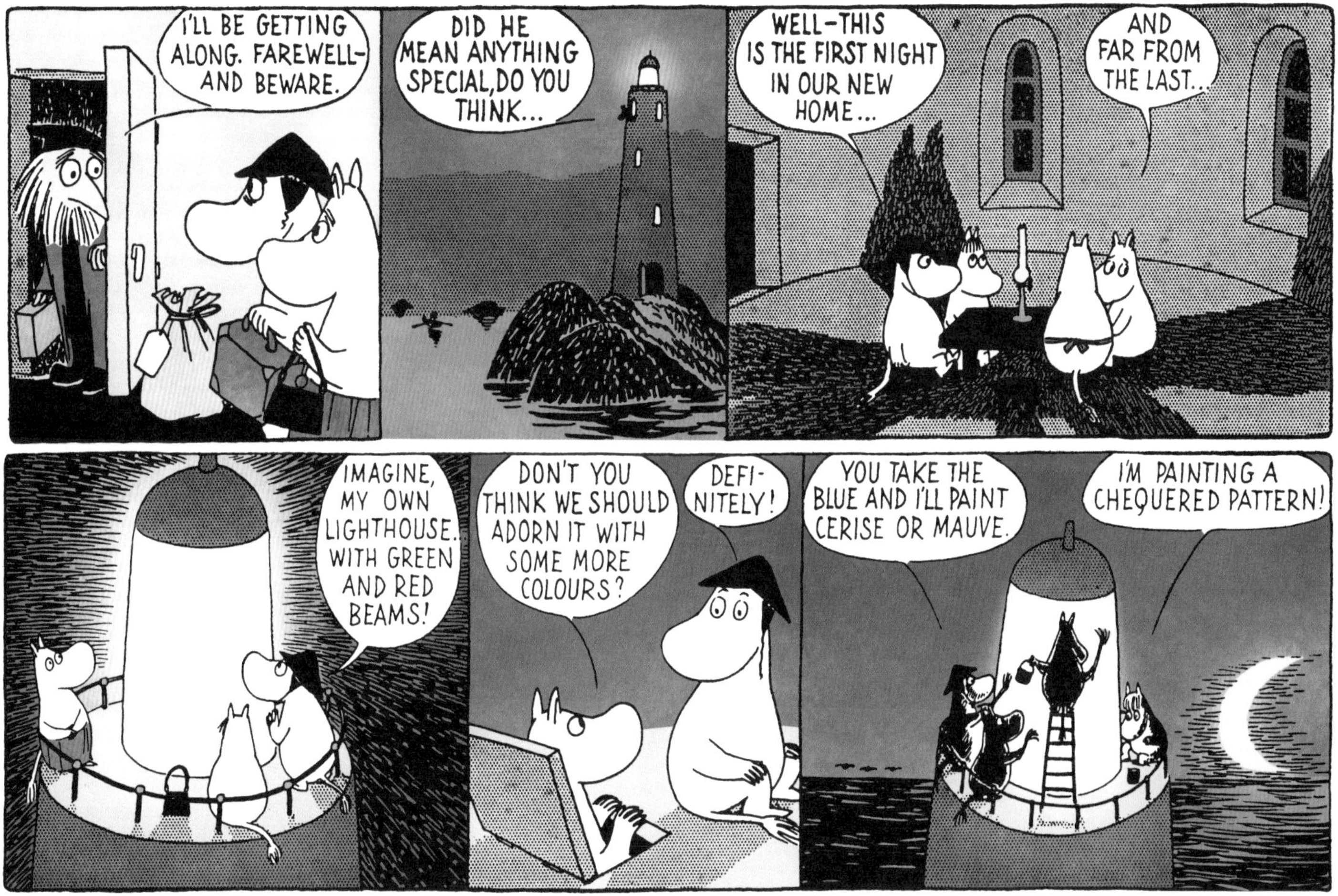
I'LL BE GETTING ALONG. FAREWELL- AND BEWARE.
DID HE MEAN ANYTHING SPECIAL, DO YOU THINK...
WELL-THIS IS THE FIRST NIGHT IN OUR NEW HOME...
AND FAR FROM THE LAST...
IMAGINE, MY OWN LIGHTHOUSE... WITH GREEN AND RED BEAMS!
DON'T YOU THINK WE SHOULD ADORN IT WITH SOME MORE COLOURS?
DEFI-NITELY!
YOU TAKE THE BLUE AND I'LL PAINT CERISE OR MAUVE.
I'M PAINTING A CHEQUERED PATTERN!

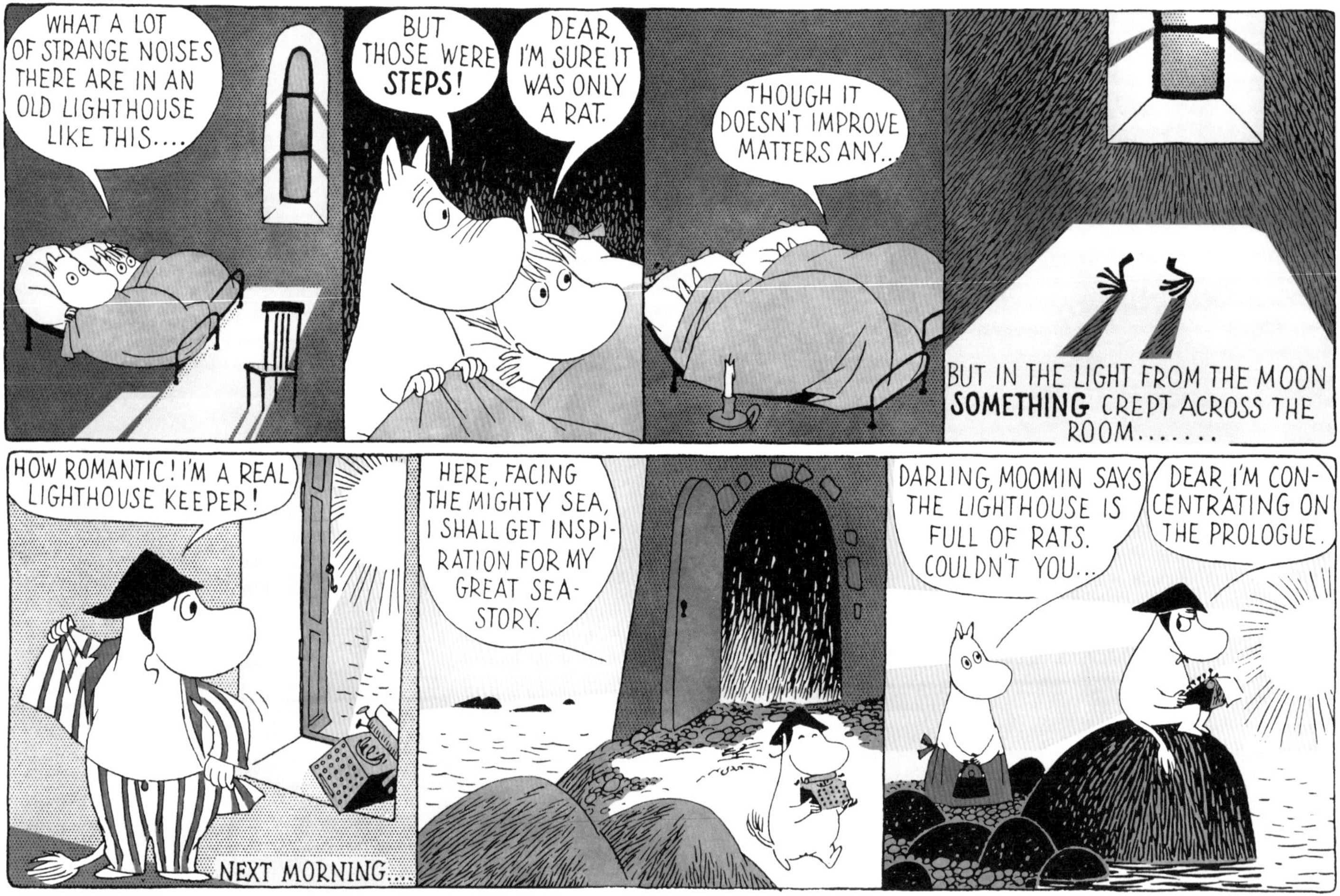
WHAT A LOT OF STRANGE NOISES THERE ARE IN AN OLD LIGHTHOUSE LIKE THIS....
BUT THOSE WERE **STEPS**!
DEAR, I'M SURE IT WAS ONLY A RAT.
THOUGH IT DOESN'T IMPROVE MATTERS ANY..
BUT IN THE LIGHT FROM THE MOON **SOMETHING** CREPT ACROSS THE ROOM.......
HOW ROMANTIC! I'M A REAL LIGHTHOUSE KEEPER!
NEXT MORNING...
HERE, FACING THE MIGHTY SEA, I SHALL GET INSPIRATION FOR MY GREAT SEA-STORY.
DARLING, MOOMIN SAYS THE LIGHTHOUSE IS FULL OF RATS. COULDN'T YOU...
DEAR, I'M CONCENTRATING ON THE PROLOGUE.

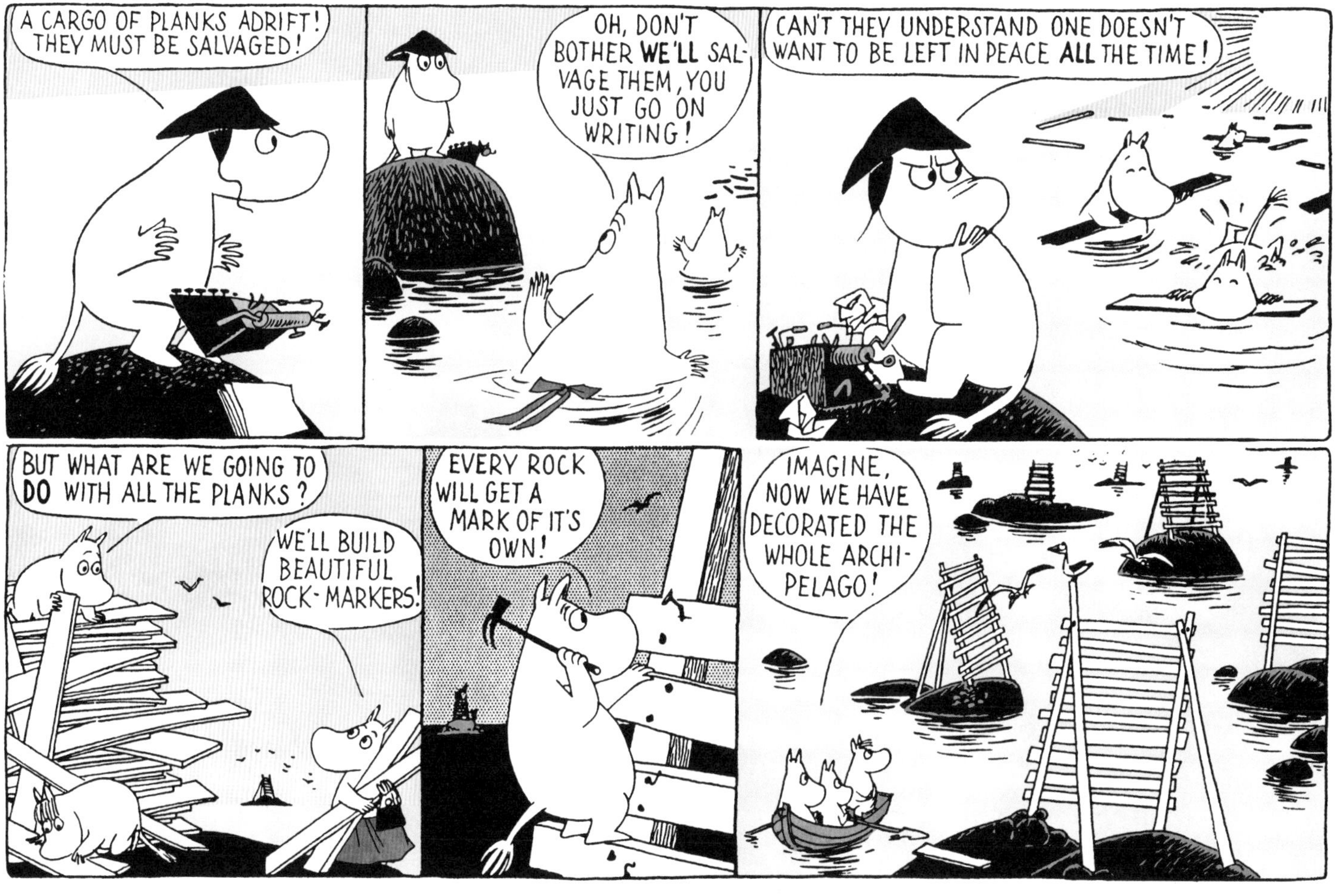
A CARGO OF PLANKS ADRIFT! THEY MUST BE SALVAGED!
OH, DON'T BOTHER **WE'LL** SAL-VAGE THEM, YOU JUST GO ON WRITING!
CAN'T THEY UNDERSTAND ONE DOESN'T WANT TO BE LEFT IN PEACE **ALL** THE TIME!
BUT WHAT ARE WE GOING TO **DO** WITH ALL THE PLANKS?
WE'LL BUILD BEAUTIFUL ROCK-MARKERS!
EVERY ROCK WILL GET A MARK OF IT'S OWN!
IMAGINE, NOW WE HAVE DECORATED THE WHOLE ARCHI-PELAGO!

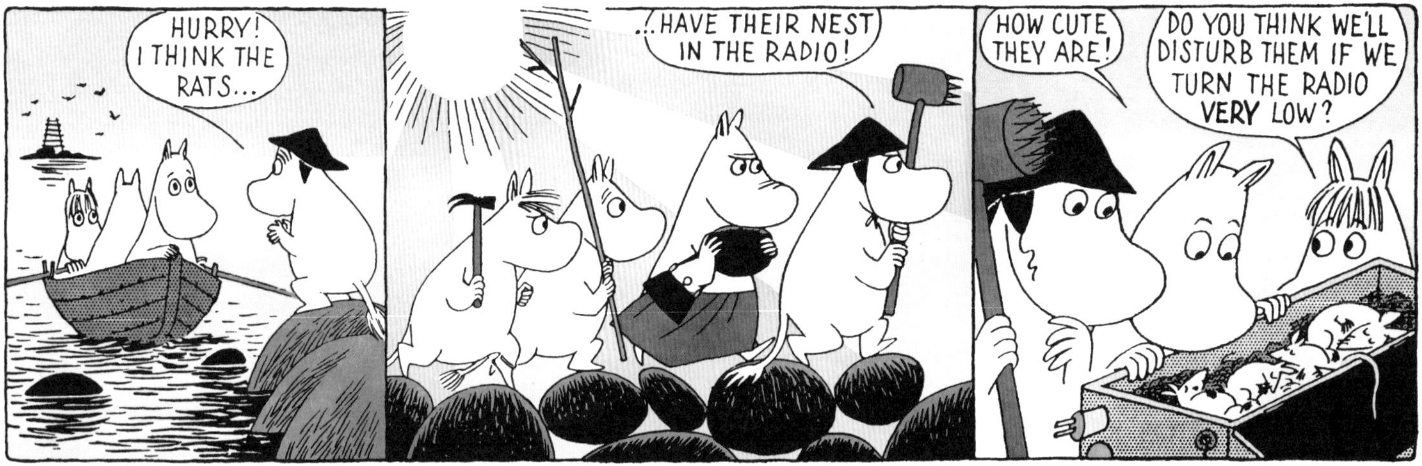
HURRY! I THINK THE RATS...
...HAVE THEIR NEST IN THE RADIO!
HOW CUTE THEY ARE!
DO YOU THINK WE'LL DISTURB THEM IF WE TURN THE RADIO **VERY** LOW?

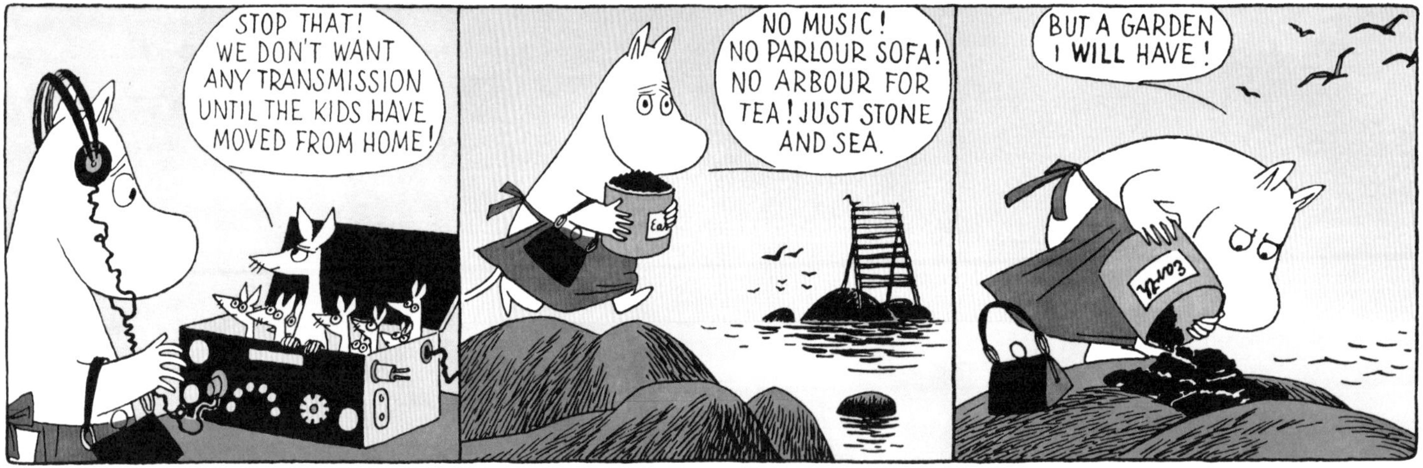
STOP THAT! WE DON'T WANT ANY TRANSMISSION UNTIL THE KIDS HAVE MOVED FROM HOME!
NO MUSIC! NO PARLOUR SOFA! NO ARBOUR FOR TEA! JUST STONE AND SEA.
BUT A GARDEN I **WILL** HAVE!

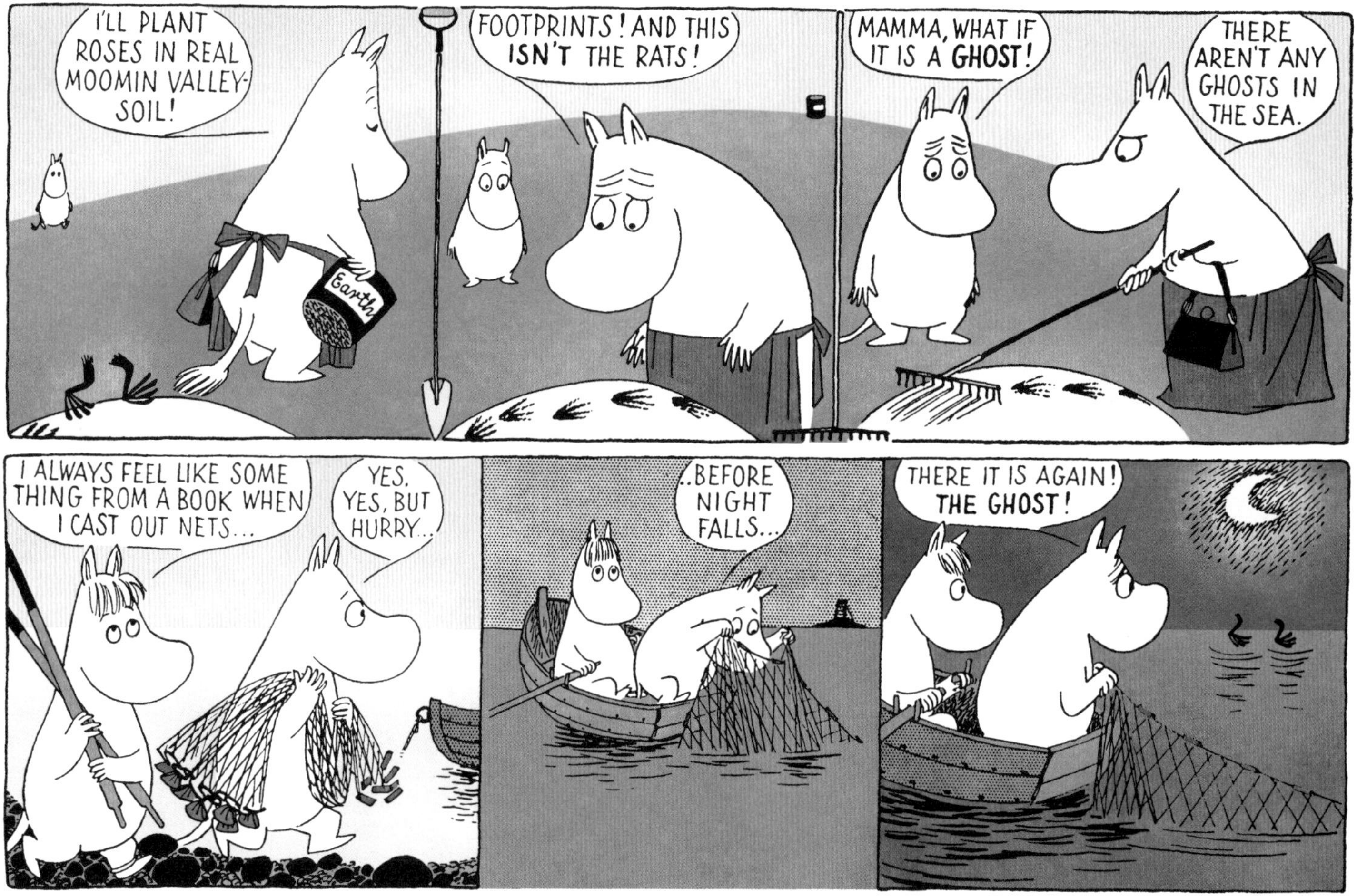
I'LL PLANT ROSES IN REAL MOOMIN VALLEY-SOIL!
Earth
FOOTPRINTS! AND THIS ISN'T THE RATS!
MAMMA, WHAT IF IT IS A GHOST!
THERE AREN'T ANY GHOSTS IN THE SEA.
I ALWAYS FEEL LIKE SOME THING FROM A BOOK WHEN I CAST OUT NETS...
YES, YES, BUT HURRY...
..BEFORE NIGHT FALLS...
THERE IT IS AGAIN! THE GHOST!

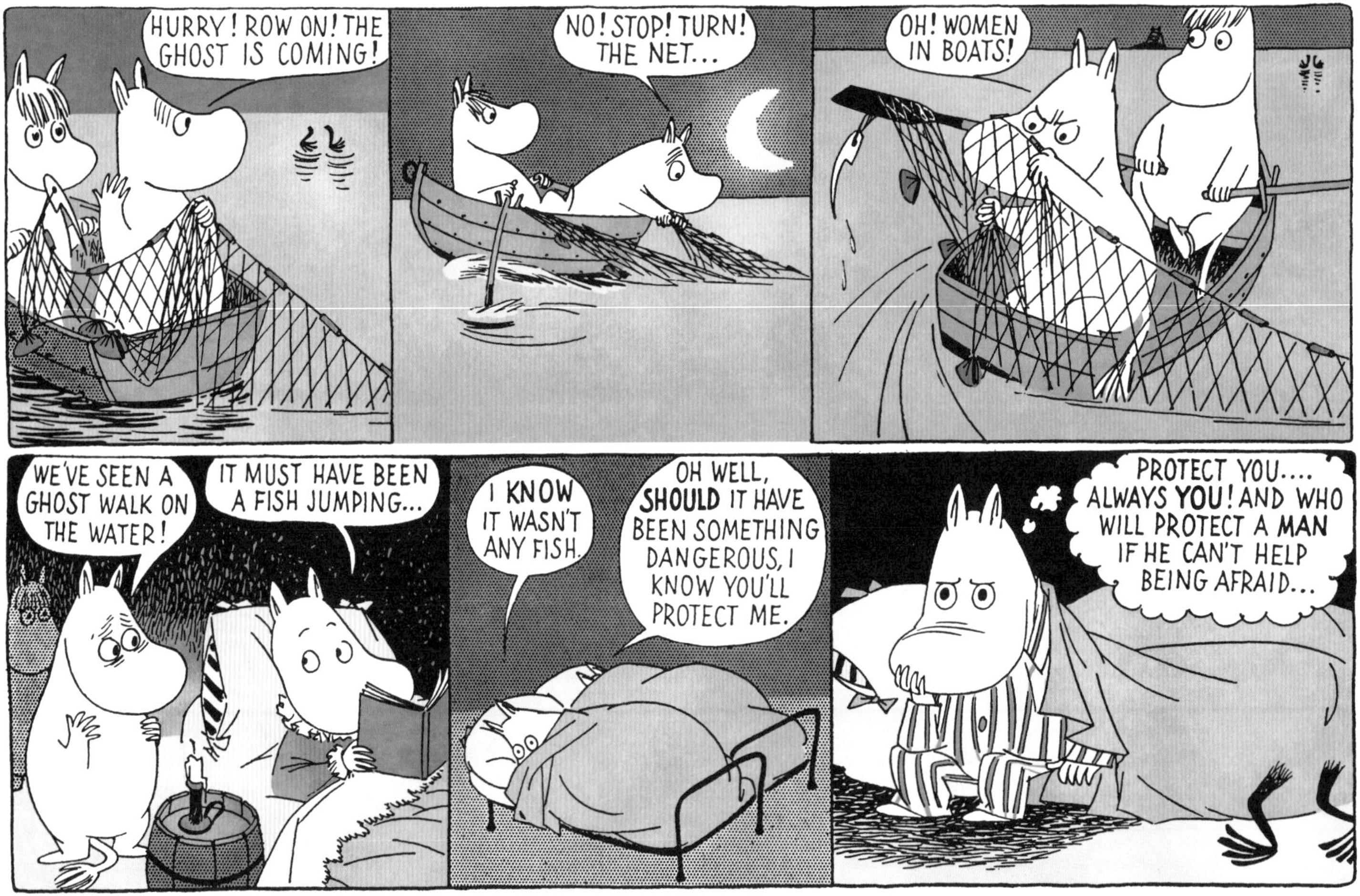
HURRY! ROW ON! THE GHOST IS COMING!
NO! STOP! TURN! THE NET...
OH! WOMEN IN BOATS!
WE'VE SEEN A GHOST WALK ON THE WATER!
IT MUST HAVE BEEN A FISH JUMPING...
I **KNOW** IT WASN'T ANY FISH.
OH WELL, **SHOULD** IT HAVE BEEN SOMETHING DANGEROUS, I KNOW YOU'LL PROTECT ME.
PROTECT YOU.... ALWAYS **YOU**! AND WHO WILL PROTECT A **MAN** IF HE CAN'T HELP BEING AFRAID...

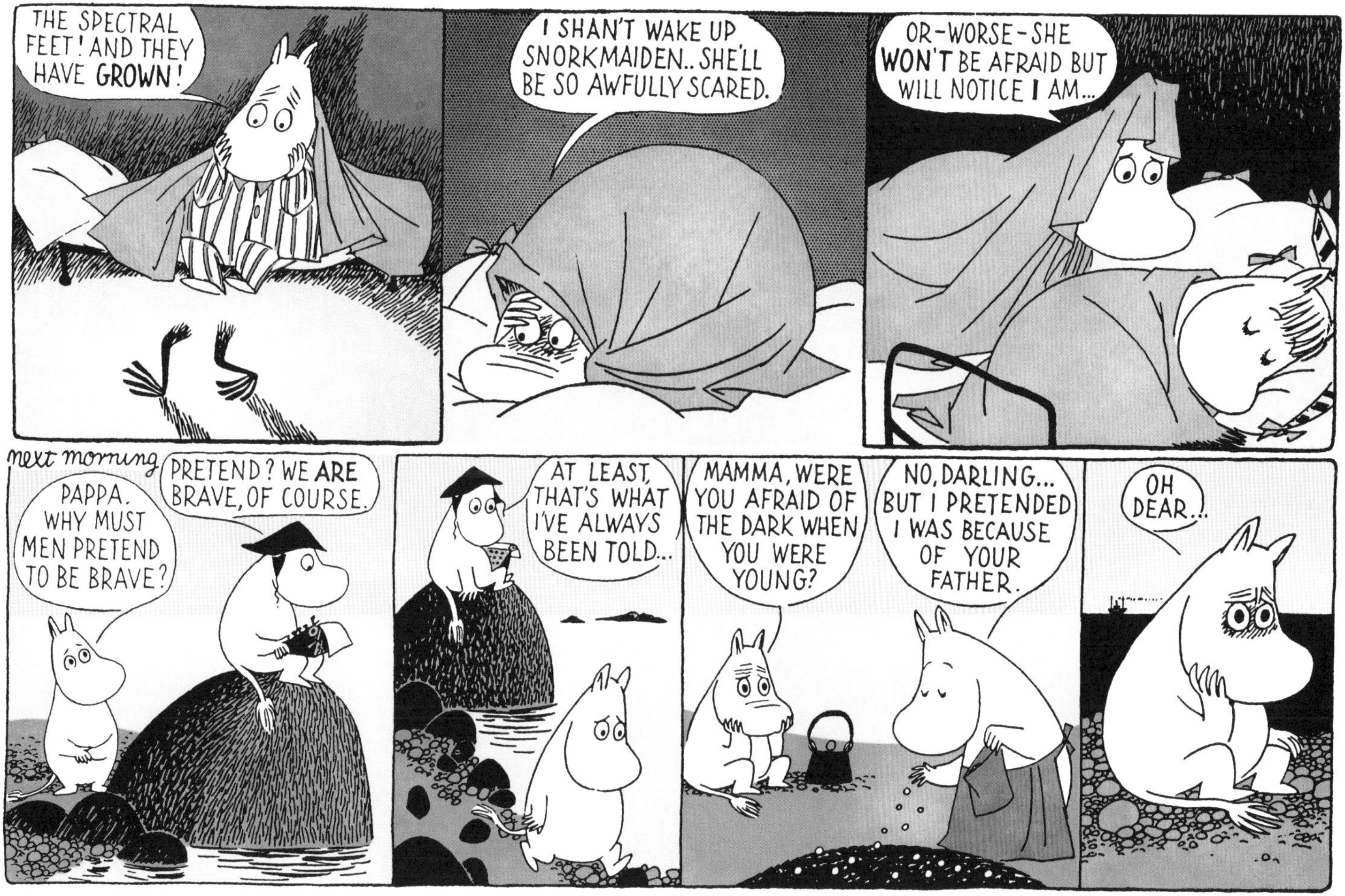
THE SPECTRAL FEET! AND THEY HAVE **GROWN**!
I SHAN'T WAKE UP SNORKMAIDEN.. SHE'LL BE SO AWFULLY SCARED.
OR-WORSE-SHE **WON'T** BE AFRAID BUT WILL NOTICE **I** AM...
next morning
PAPPA. WHY MUST MEN PRETEND TO BE BRAVE?
PRETEND? WE **ARE** BRAVE, OF COURSE.
AT LEAST, THAT'S WHAT I'VE ALWAYS BEEN TOLD...
MAMMA, WERE YOU AFRAID OF THE DARK WHEN YOU WERE YOUNG?
NO, DARLING... BUT I PRETENDED I WAS BECAUSE OF YOUR FATHER.
OH DEAR...

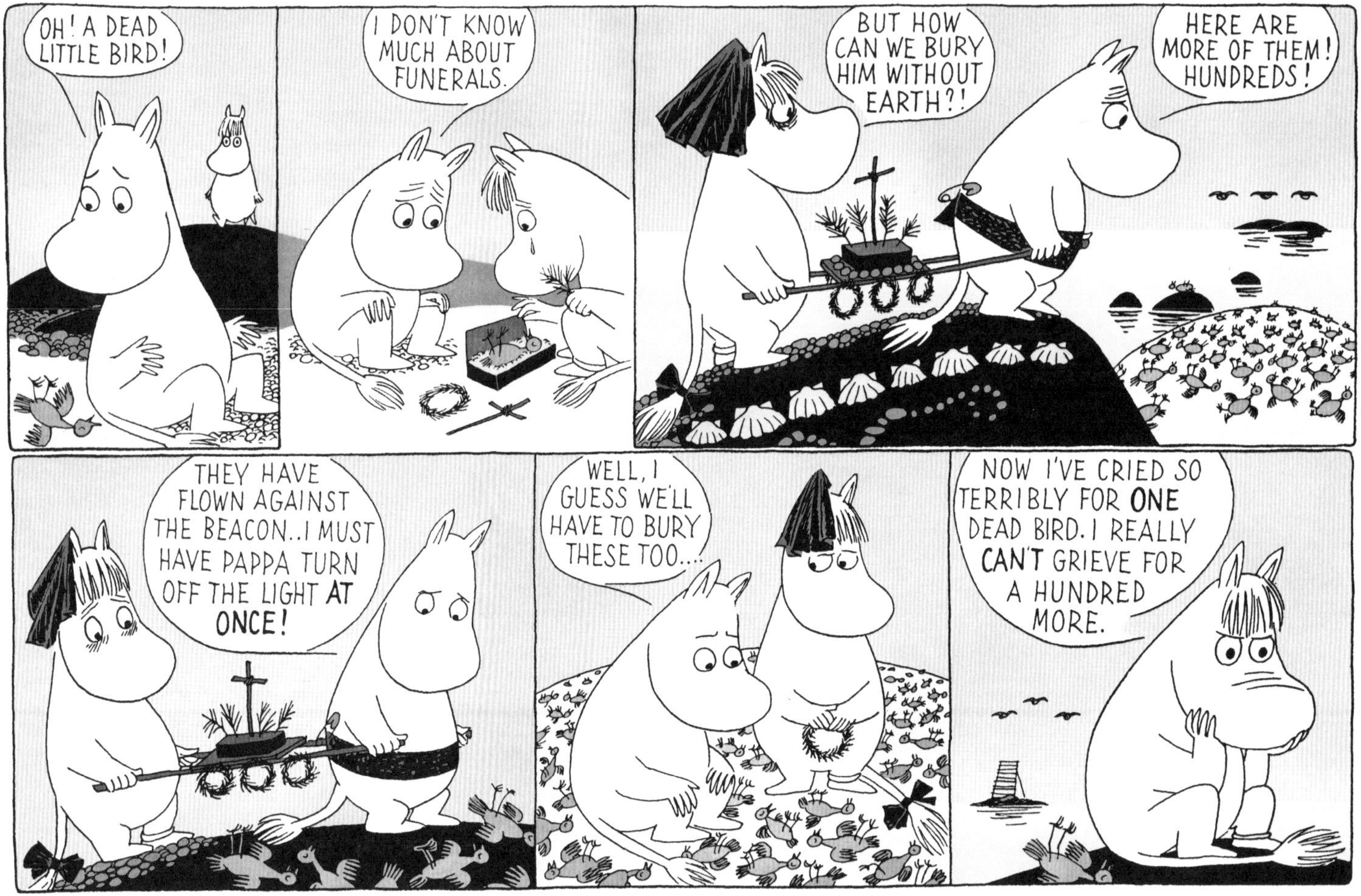

OH! A DEAD LITTLE BIRD!
I DON'T KNOW MUCH ABOUT FUNERALS.
BUT HOW CAN WE BURY HIM WITHOUT EARTH?!
HERE ARE MORE OF THEM! HUNDREDS!
THEY HAVE FLOWN AGAINST THE BEACON..I MUST HAVE PAPPA TURN OFF THE LIGHT AT ONCE!
WELL, I GUESS WE'LL HAVE TO BURY THESE TOO...
NOW I'VE CRIED SO TERRIBLY FOR ONE DEAD BIRD. I REALLY CAN'T GRIEVE FOR A HUNDRED MORE.

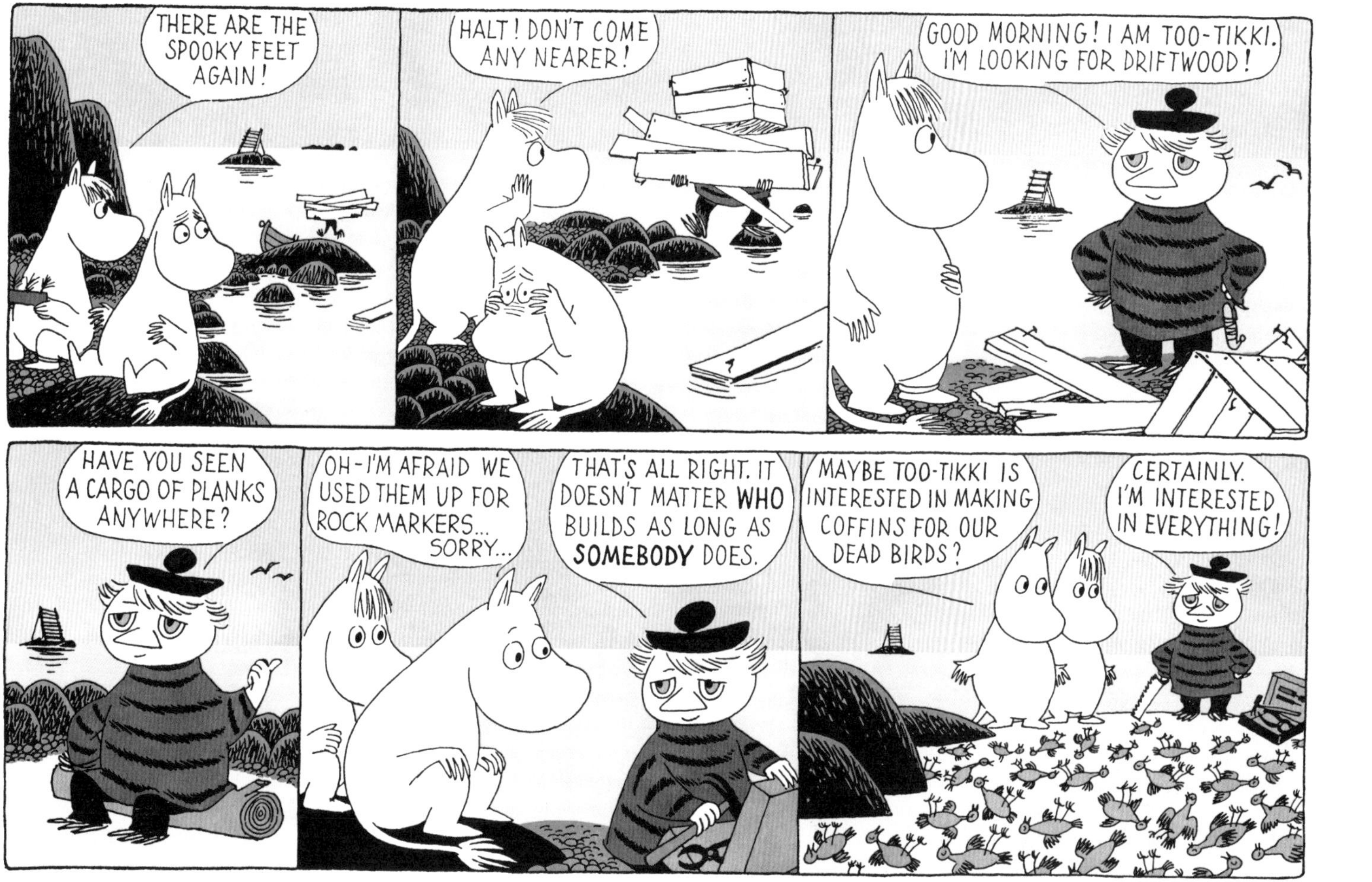
THERE ARE THE SPOOKY FEET AGAIN!
HALT! DON'T COME ANY NEARER!
GOOD MORNING! I AM TOO-TIKKI. I'M LOOKING FOR DRIFTWOOD!
HAVE YOU SEEN A CARGO OF PLANKS ANYWHERE?
OH-I'M AFRAID WE USED THEM UP FOR ROCK MARKERS... SORRY...
THAT'S ALL RIGHT. IT DOESN'T MATTER **WHO** BUILDS AS LONG AS **SOMEBODY** DOES.
MAYBE TOO-TIKKI IS INTERESTED IN MAKING COFFINS FOR OUR DEAD BIRDS?
CERTAINLY. I'M INTERESTED IN EVERYTHING!

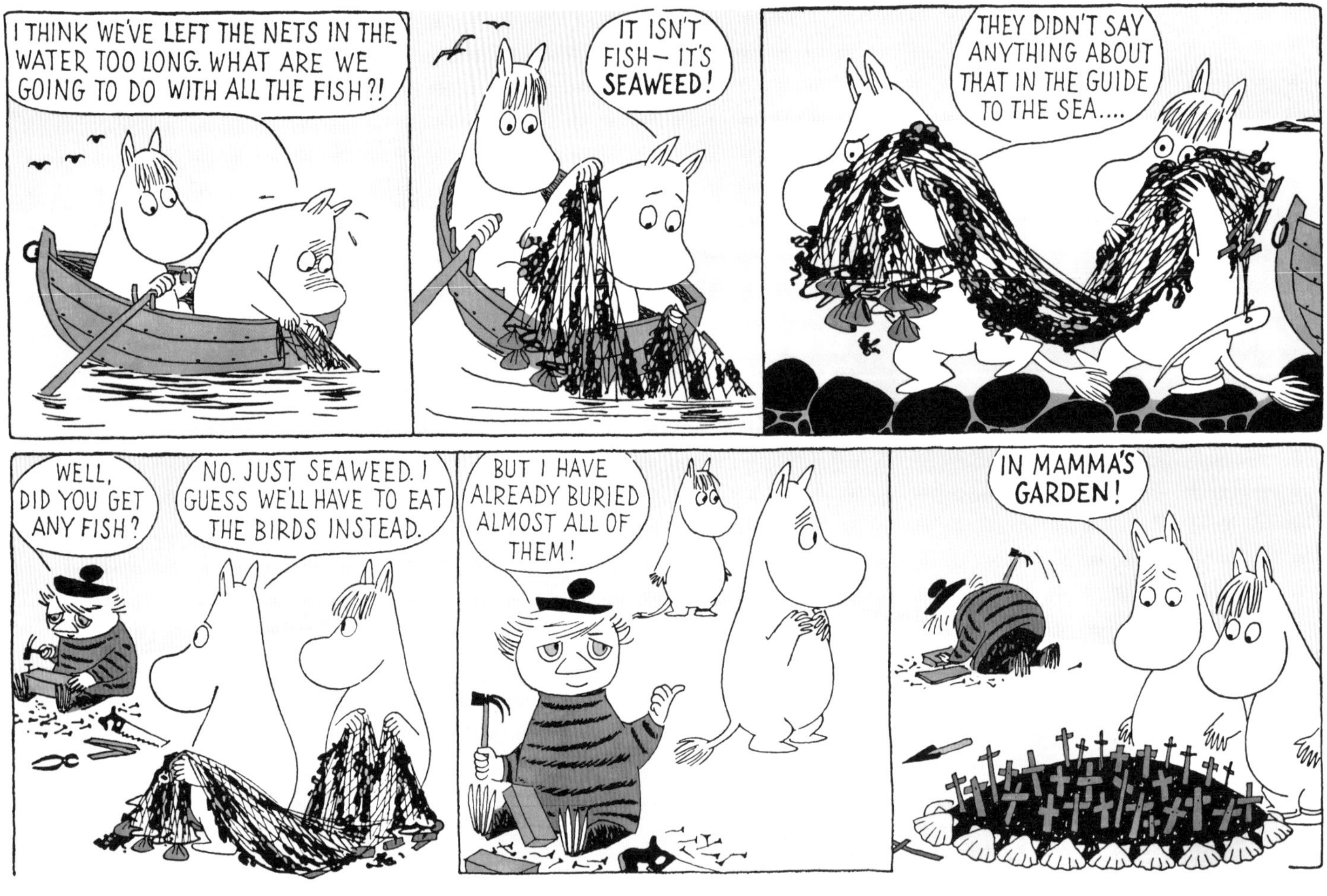
I THINK WE'VE LEFT THE NETS IN THE WATER TOO LONG. WHAT ARE WE GOING TO DO WITH ALL THE FISH?!
IT ISN'T FISH – IT'S SEAWEED!
THEY DIDN'T SAY ANYTHING ABOUT THAT IN THE GUIDE TO THE SEA....
WELL, DID YOU GET ANY FISH?
NO. JUST SEAWEED. I GUESS WE'LL HAVE TO EAT THE BIRDS INSTEAD.
BUT I HAVE ALREADY BURIED ALMOST ALL OF THEM!
IN MAMMA'S GARDEN!

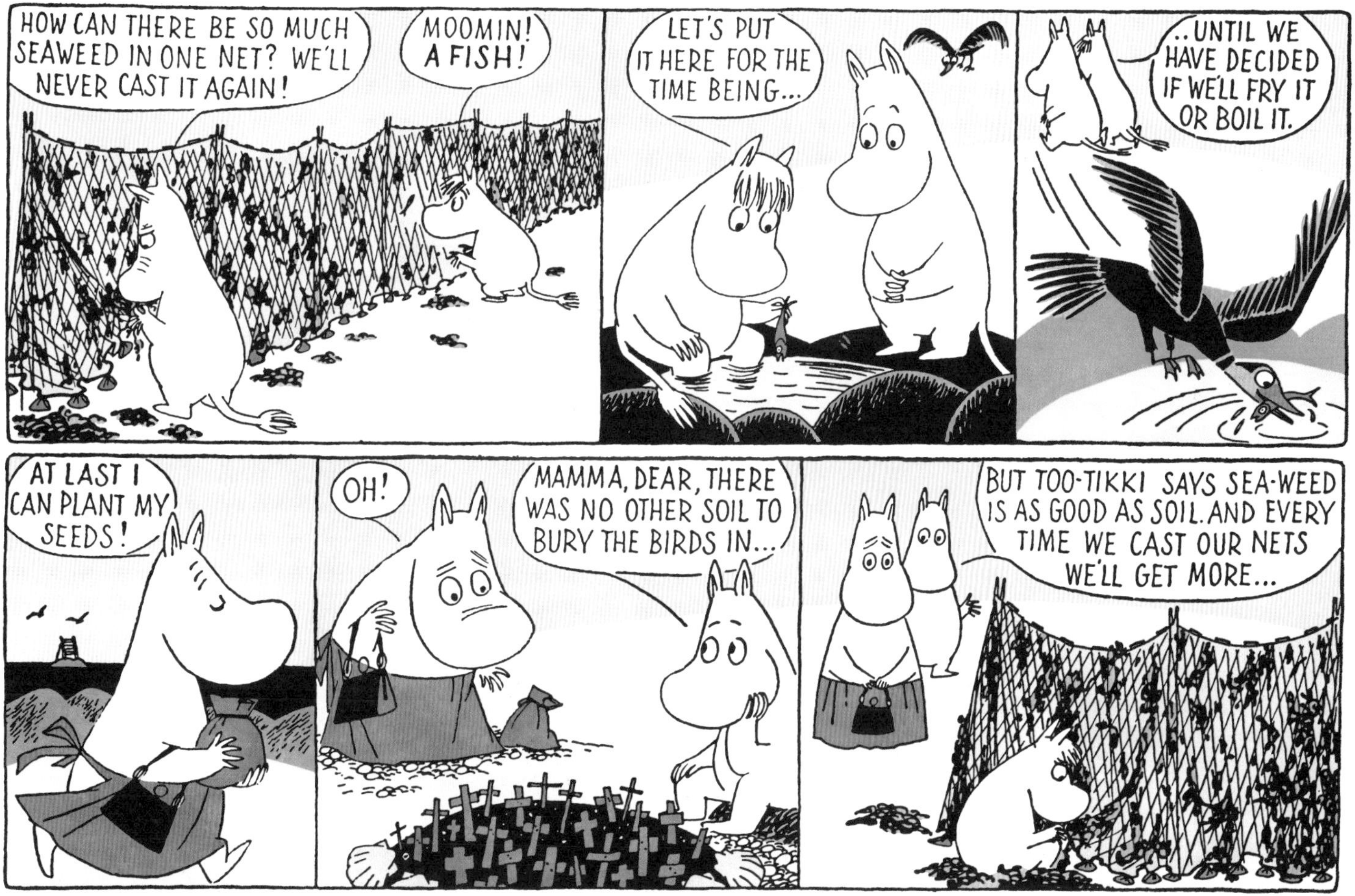
HOW CAN THERE BE SO MUCH SEAWEED IN ONE NET? WE'LL NEVER CAST IT AGAIN!
MOOMIN! A FISH!
LET'S PUT IT HERE FOR THE TIME BEING...
..UNTIL WE HAVE DECIDED IF WE'LL FRY IT OR BOIL IT.
AT LAST I CAN PLANT MY SEEDS!
OH!
MAMMA, DEAR, THERE WAS NO OTHER SOIL TO BURY THE BIRDS IN...
BUT TOO-TIKKI SAYS SEA-WEED IS AS GOOD AS SOIL. AND EVERY TIME WE CAST OUR NETS WE'LL GET MORE...

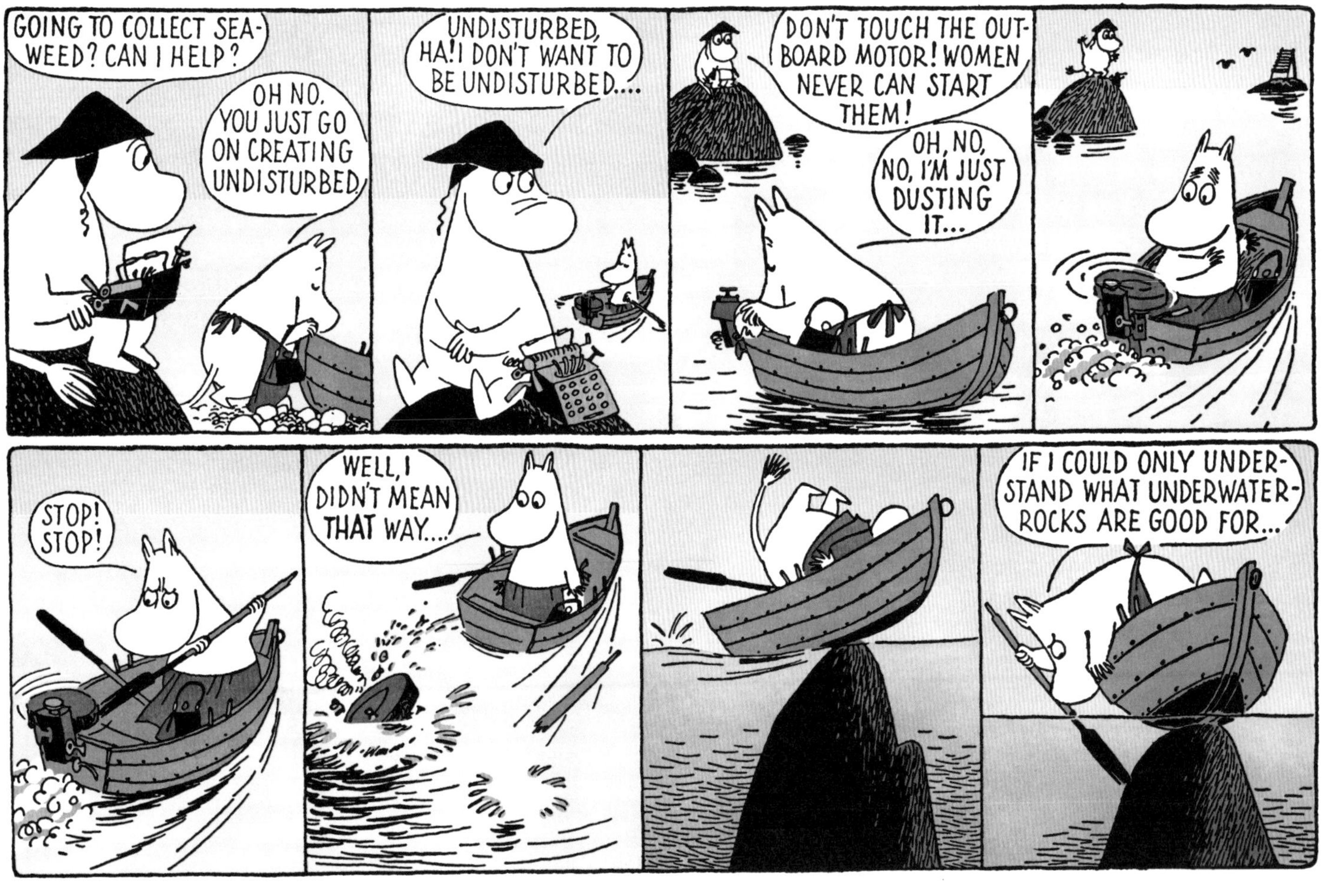
GOING TO COLLECT SEA-WEED? CAN I HELP?
OH NO. YOU JUST GO ON CREATING UNDISTURBED.
UNDISTURBED, HA! I DON'T WANT TO BE UNDISTURBED....
DON'T TOUCH THE OUT-BOARD MOTOR! WOMEN NEVER CAN START THEM!
OH, NO, NO, I'M JUST DUSTING IT...
STOP! STOP!
WELL, I DIDN'T MEAN THAT WAY....
IF I COULD ONLY UNDER-STAND WHAT UNDERWATER-ROCKS ARE GOOD FOR...

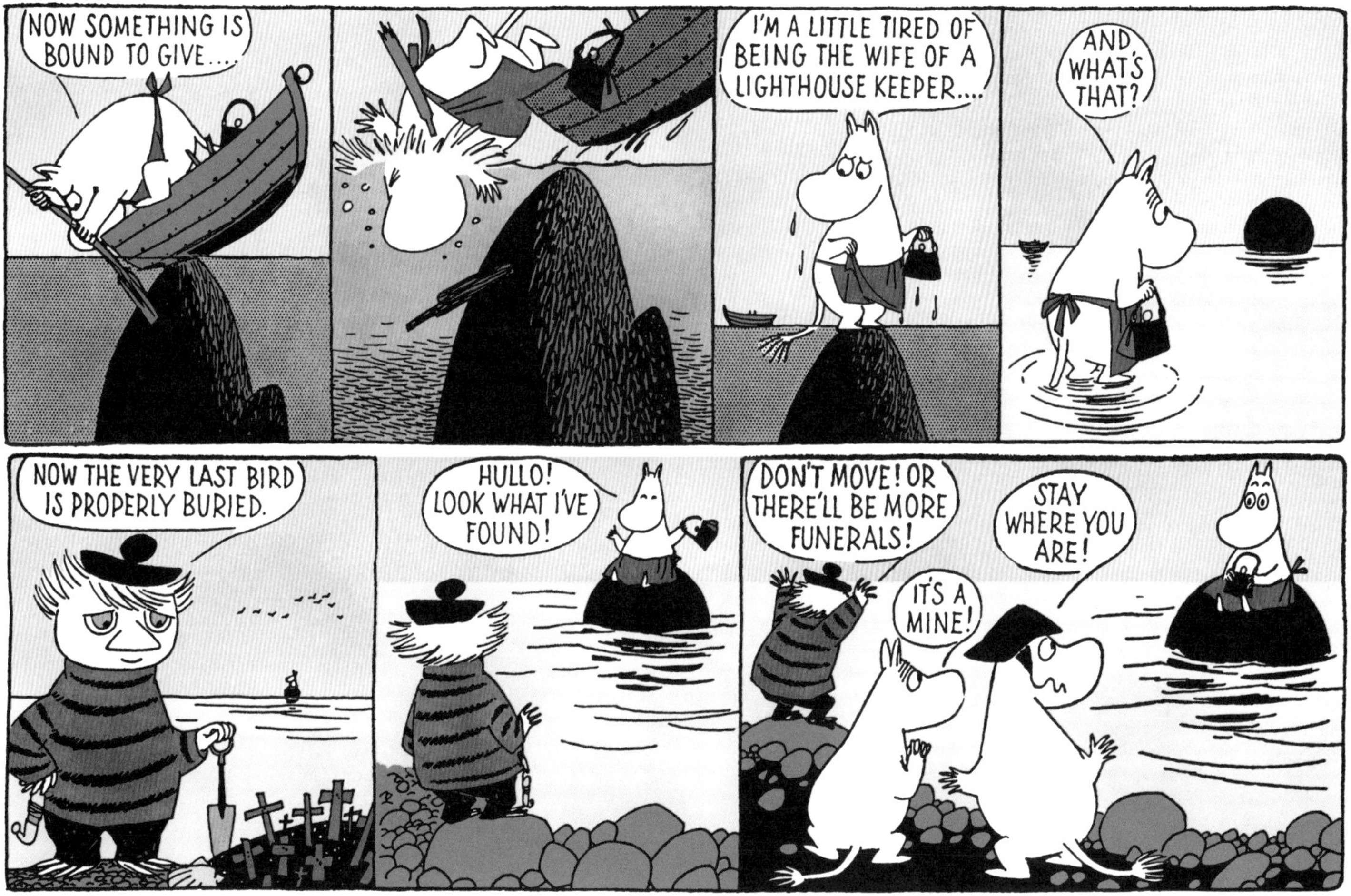
NOW SOMETHING IS BOUND TO GIVE....
I'M A LITTLE TIRED OF BEING THE WIFE OF A LIGHTHOUSE KEEPER....
AND WHAT'S THAT?
NOW THE VERY LAST BIRD IS PROPERLY BURIED.
HULLO! LOOK WHAT I'VE FOUND!
DON'T MOVE! OR THERE'LL BE MORE FUNERALS!
STAY WHERE YOU ARE!
IT'S A MINE!

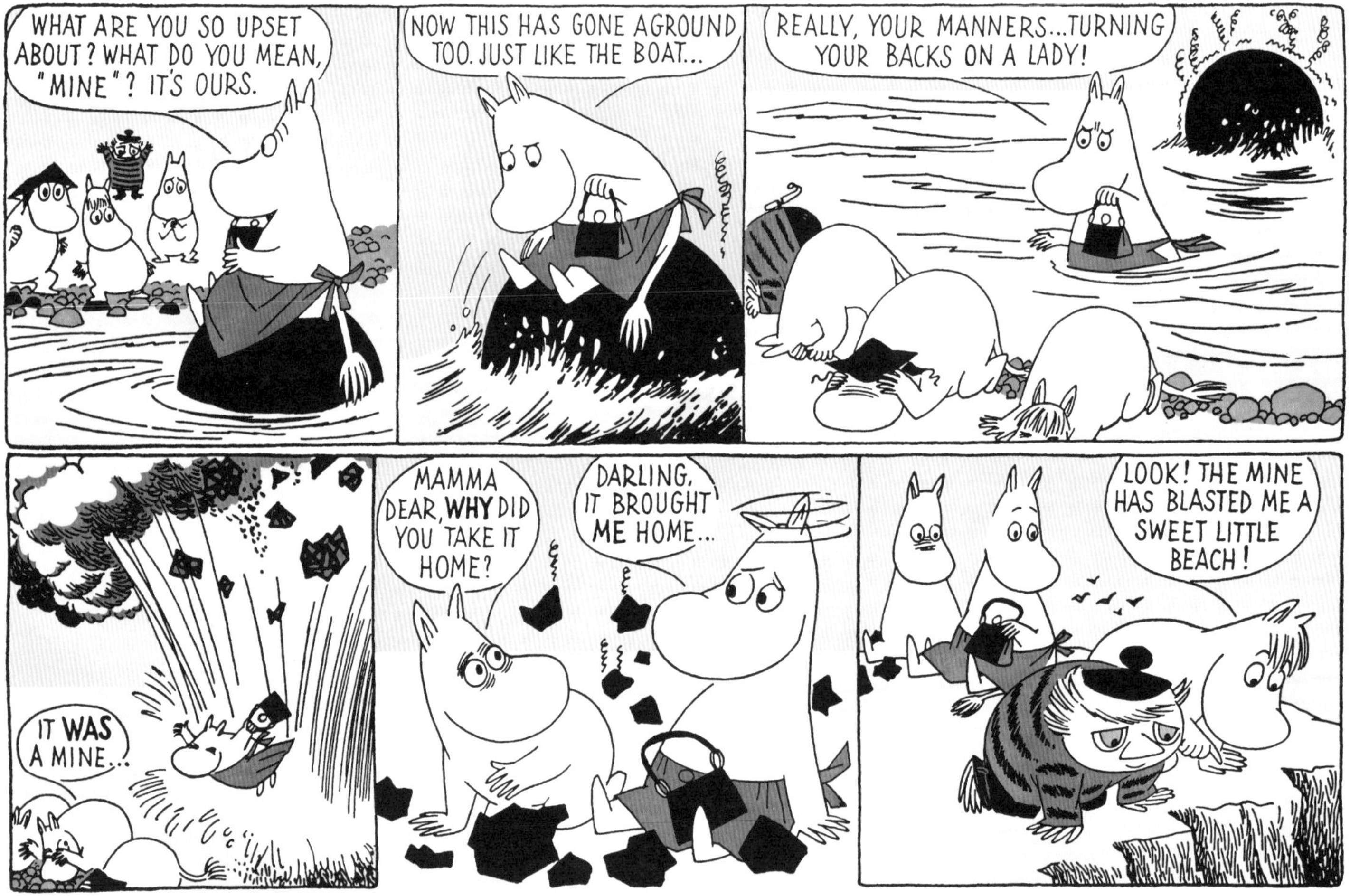
WHAT ARE YOU SO UPSET ABOUT? WHAT DO YOU MEAN, "MINE"? IT'S OURS.
NOW THIS HAS GONE AGROUND TOO. JUST LIKE THE BOAT...
REALLY, YOUR MANNERS...TURNING YOUR BACKS ON A LADY!
IT WAS A MINE...
MAMMA DEAR, WHY DID YOU TAKE IT HOME?
DARLING, IT BROUGHT ME HOME...
LOOK! THE MINE HAS BLASTED ME A SWEET LITTLE BEACH!

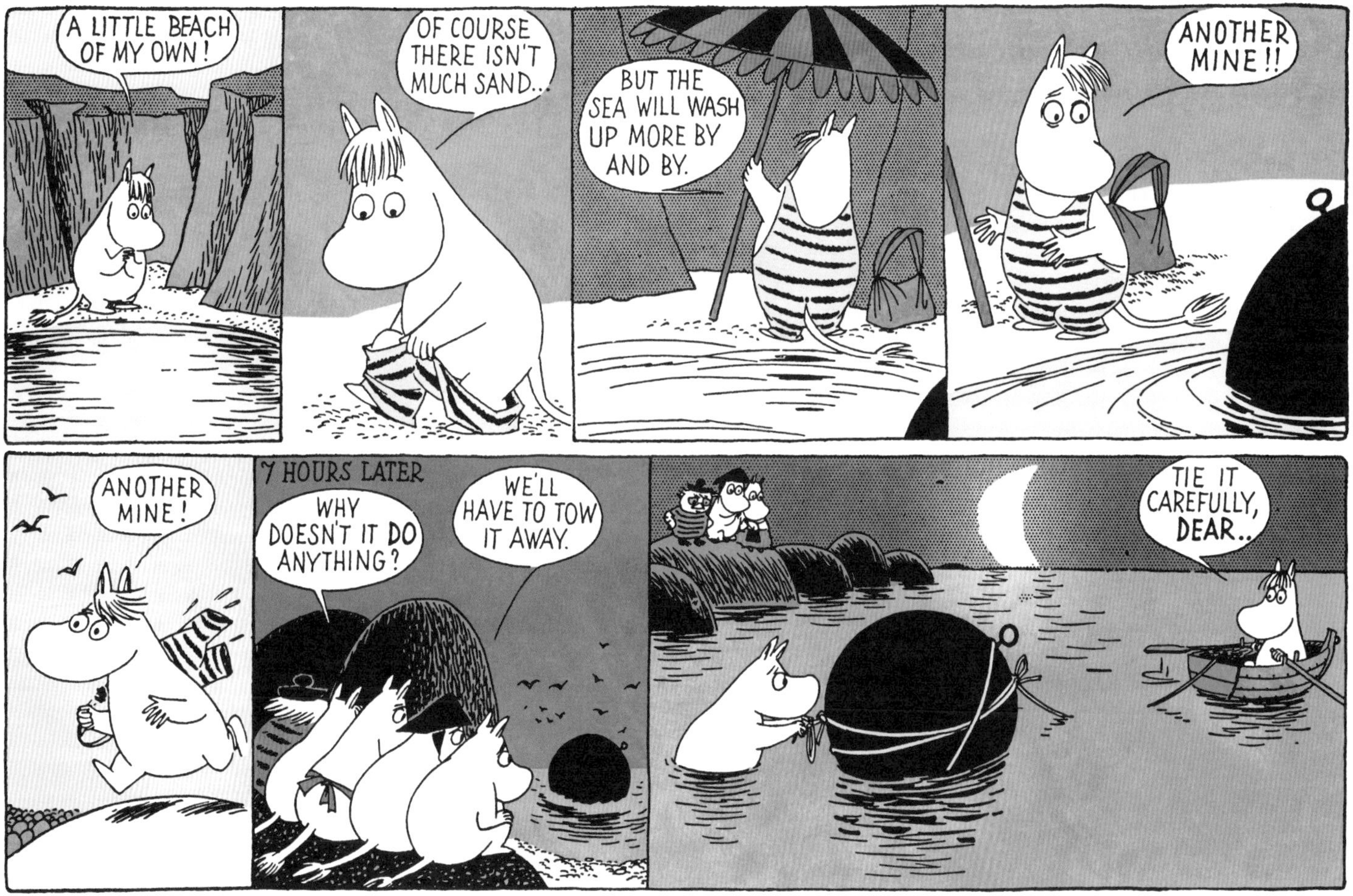
A LITTLE BEACH OF MY OWN!
OF COURSE THERE ISN'T MUCH SAND..
BUT THE SEA WILL WASH UP MORE BY AND BY.
ANOTHER MINE!!
ANOTHER MINE!
7 HOURS LATER
WHY DOESN'T IT DO ANYTHING?
WE'LL HAVE TO TOW IT AWAY.
TIE IT CAREFULLY, DEAR..

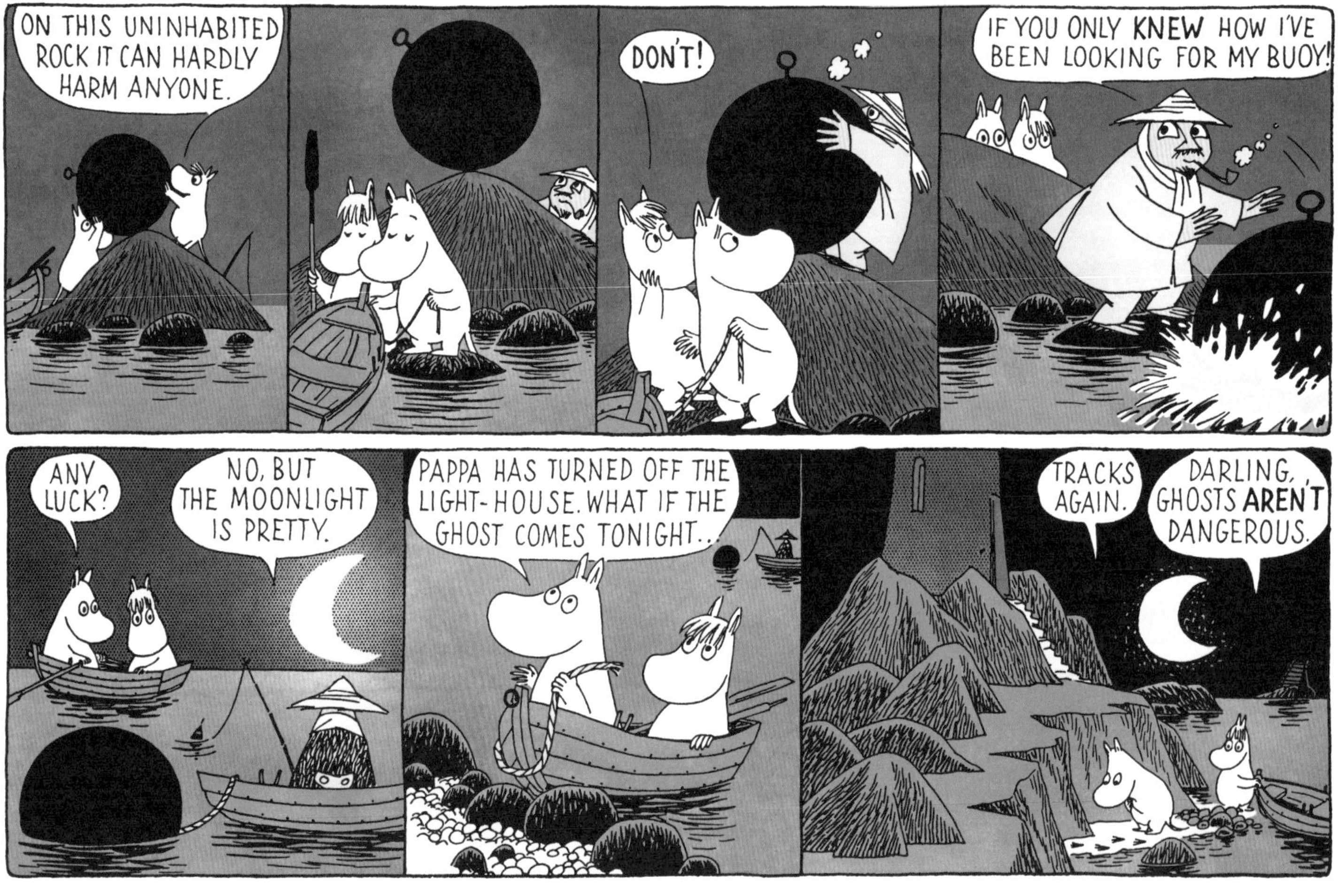
ON THIS UNINHABITED ROCK IT CAN HARDLY HARM ANYONE.
DON'T!
IF YOU ONLY **KNEW** HOW I'VE BEEN LOOKING FOR MY BUOY!
ANY LUCK?
NO, BUT THE MOONLIGHT IS PRETTY.
PAPPA HAS TURNED OFF THE LIGHT-HOUSE. WHAT IF THE GHOST COMES TONIGHT...
TRACKS AGAIN.
DARLING, GHOSTS **AREN'T** DANGEROUS.

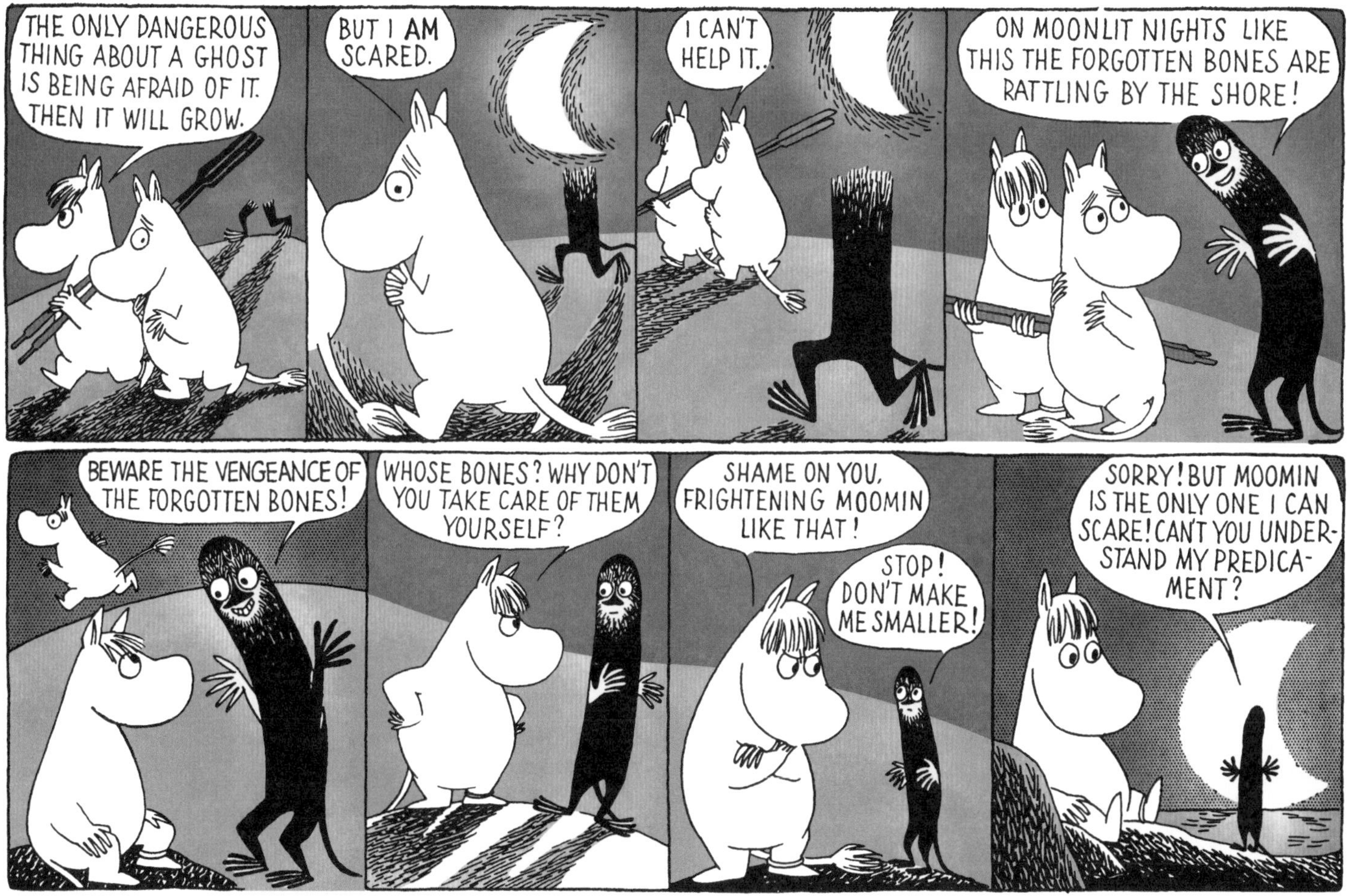
THE ONLY DANGEROUS THING ABOUT A GHOST IS BEING AFRAID OF IT. THEN IT WILL GROW.
BUT I AM SCARED.
I CAN'T HELP IT...
ON MOONLIT NIGHTS LIKE THIS THE FORGOTTEN BONES ARE RATTLING BY THE SHORE!
BEWARE THE VENGEANCE OF THE FORGOTTEN BONES!
WHOSE BONES? WHY DON'T YOU TAKE CARE OF THEM YOURSELF?
SHAME ON YOU, FRIGHTENING MOOMIN LIKE THAT!
STOP! DON'T MAKE ME SMALLER!
SORRY! BUT MOOMIN IS THE ONLY ONE I CAN SCARE! CAN'T YOU UNDERSTAND MY PREDICAMENT?

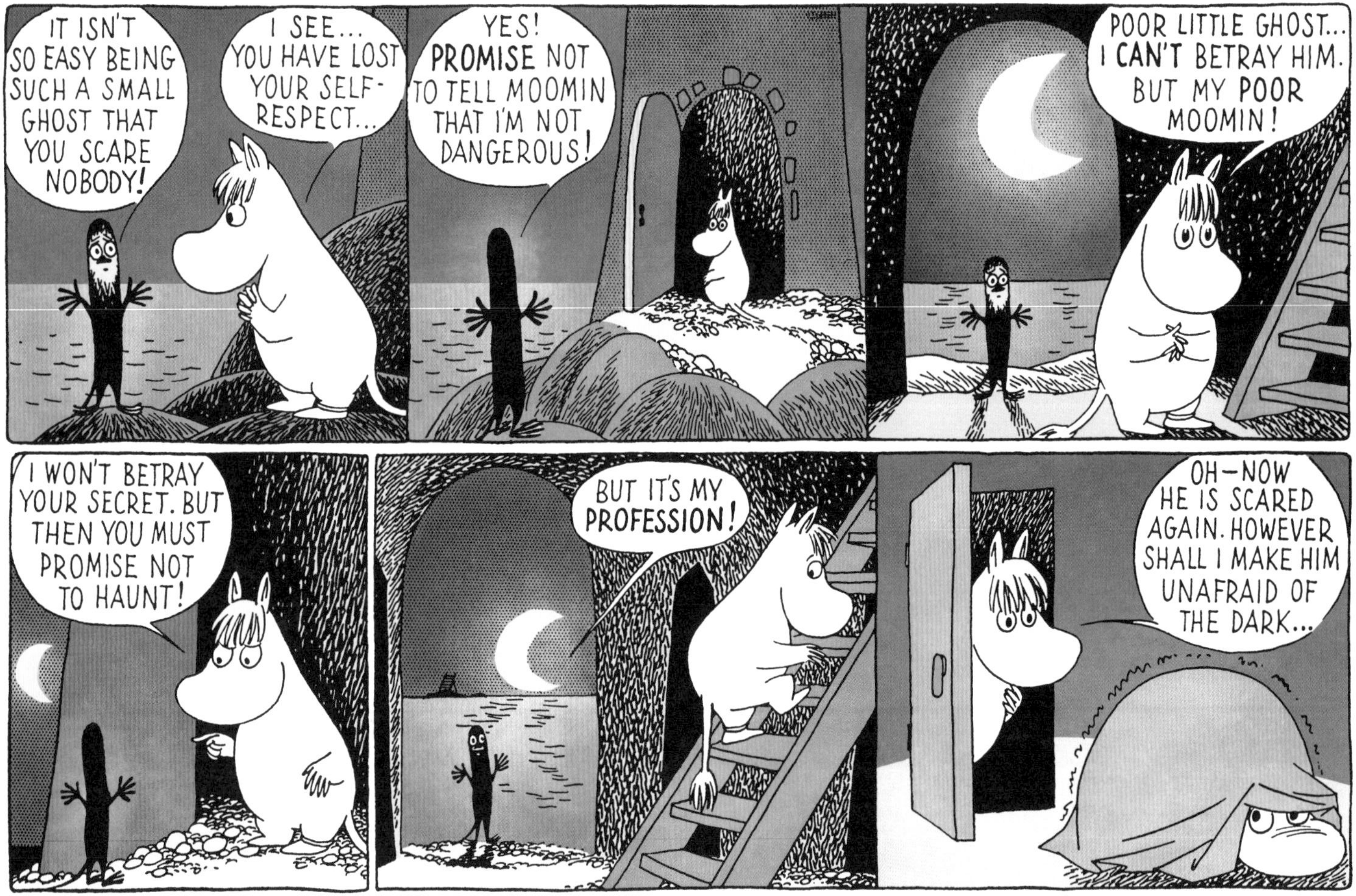
IT ISN'T SO EASY BEING SUCH A SMALL GHOST THAT YOU SCARE NOBODY!
I SEE... YOU HAVE LOST YOUR SELF-RESPECT...
YES! PROMISE NOT TO TELL MOOMIN THAT I'M NOT DANGEROUS!
POOR LITTLE GHOST... I CAN'T BETRAY HIM. BUT MY POOR MOOMIN!
I WON'T BETRAY YOUR SECRET. BUT THEN YOU MUST PROMISE NOT TO HAUNT!
BUT IT'S MY PROFESSION!
OH—NOW HE IS SCARED AGAIN. HOWEVER SHALL I MAKE HIM UNAFRAID OF THE DARK...

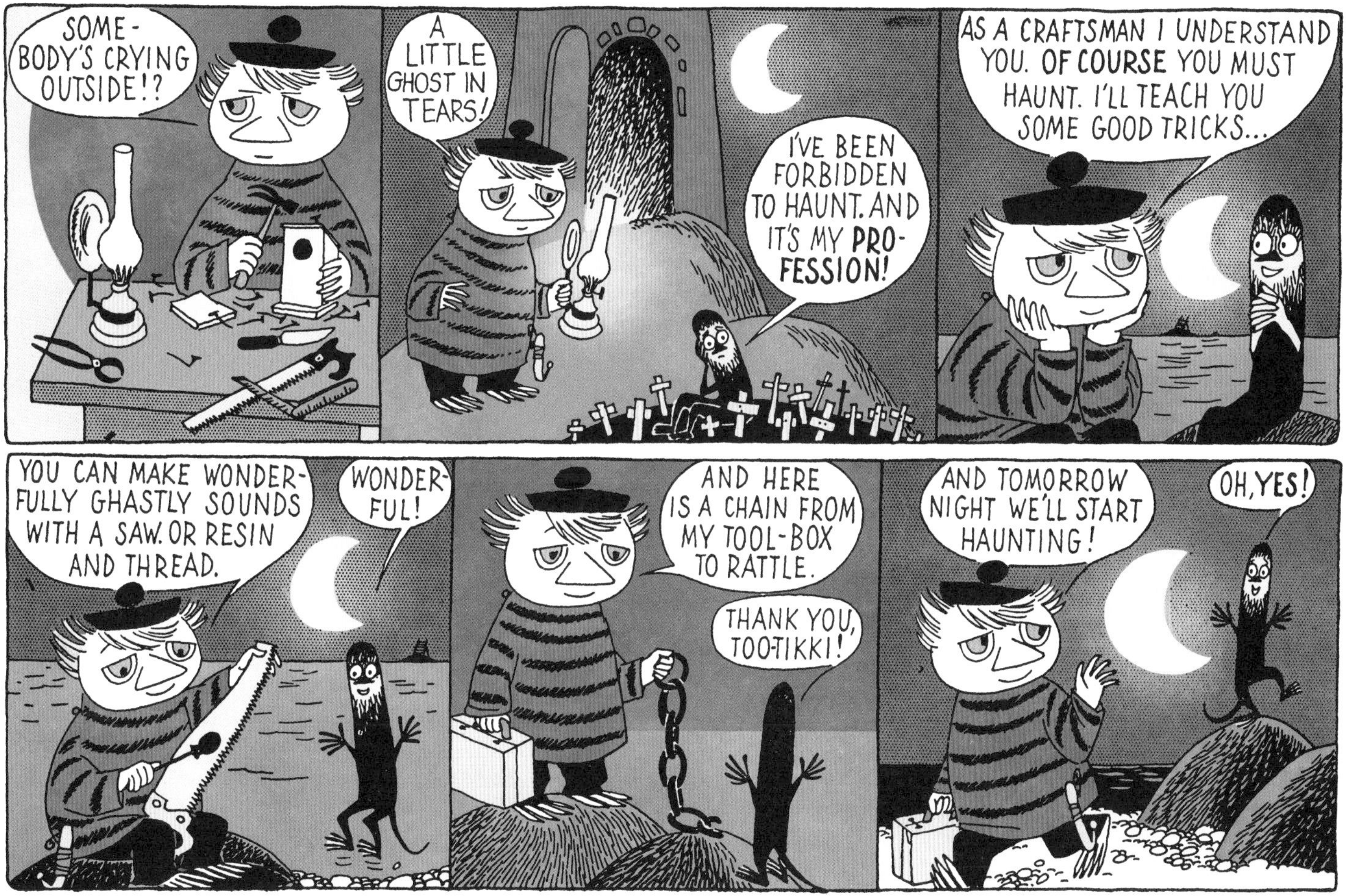
SOME-BODY'S CRYING OUTSIDE!?
A LITTLE GHOST IN TEARS!
I'VE BEEN FORBIDDEN TO HAUNT. AND IT'S MY **PRO-FESSION!**
AS A CRAFTSMAN I UNDERSTAND YOU. **OF COURSE** YOU MUST HAUNT. I'LL TEACH YOU SOME GOOD TRICKS...
YOU CAN MAKE WONDER-FULLY GHASTLY SOUNDS WITH A SAW. OR RESIN AND THREAD.
WONDER-FUL!
AND HERE IS A CHAIN FROM MY TOOL-BOX TO RATTLE.
THANK YOU, TOO-TIKKI!
AND TOMORROW NIGHT WE'LL START HAUNTING!
OH, **YES!**

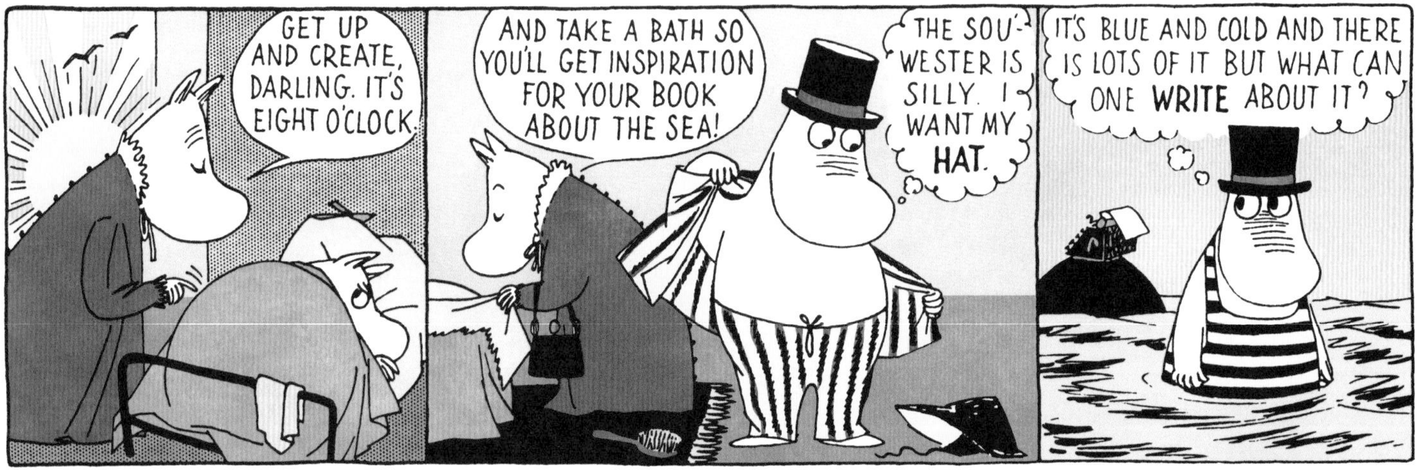
GET UP AND CREATE, DARLING. IT'S EIGHT O'CLOCK.
AND TAKE A BATH SO YOU'LL GET INSPIRATION FOR YOUR BOOK ABOUT THE SEA!
THE SOU'-WESTER IS SILLY. I WANT MY **HAT**.
IT'S BLUE AND COLD AND THERE IS LOTS OF IT BUT WHAT CAN ONE **WRITE** ABOUT IT?

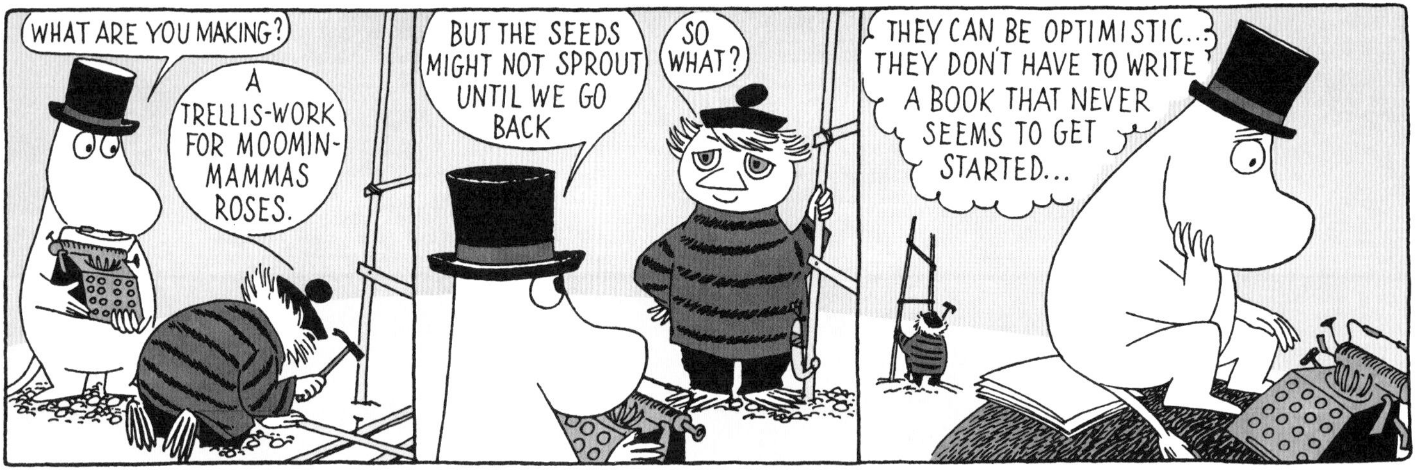
WHAT ARE YOU MAKING?
A TRELLIS-WORK FOR MOOMIN-MAMMAS ROSES.
BUT THE SEEDS MIGHT NOT SPROUT UNTIL WE GO BACK
SO WHAT?
THEY CAN BE OPTIMISTIC... THEY DON'T HAVE TO WRITE A BOOK THAT NEVER SEEMS TO GET STARTED...

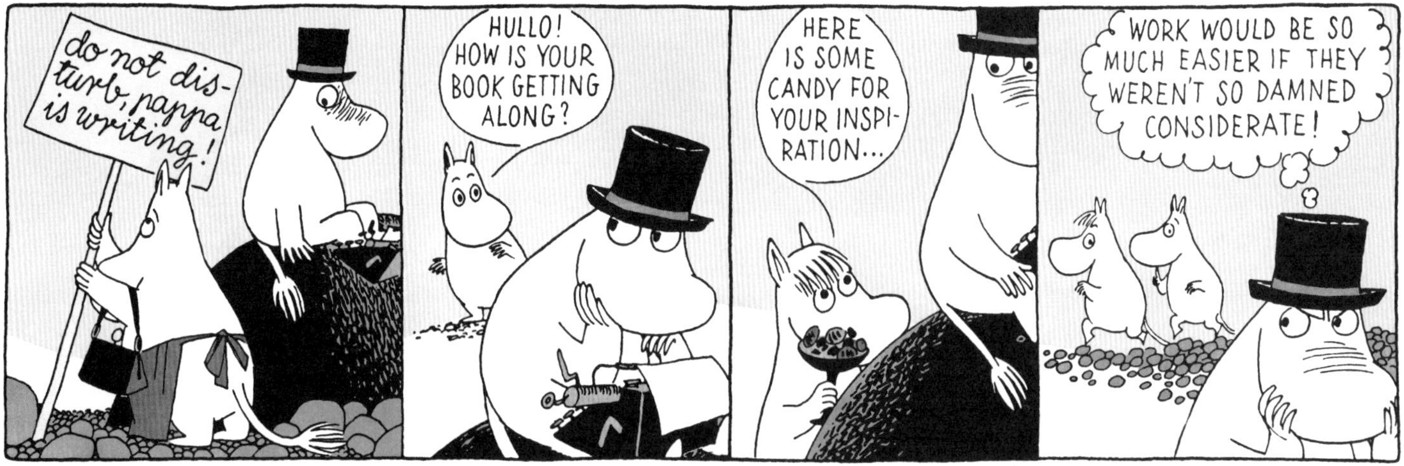
do not disturb, pappa is writing!
HULLO! HOW IS YOUR BOOK GETTING ALONG?
HERE IS SOME CANDY FOR YOUR INSPIRATION...
WORK WOULD BE SO MUCH EASIER IF THEY WEREN'T SO DAMNED CONSIDERATE!

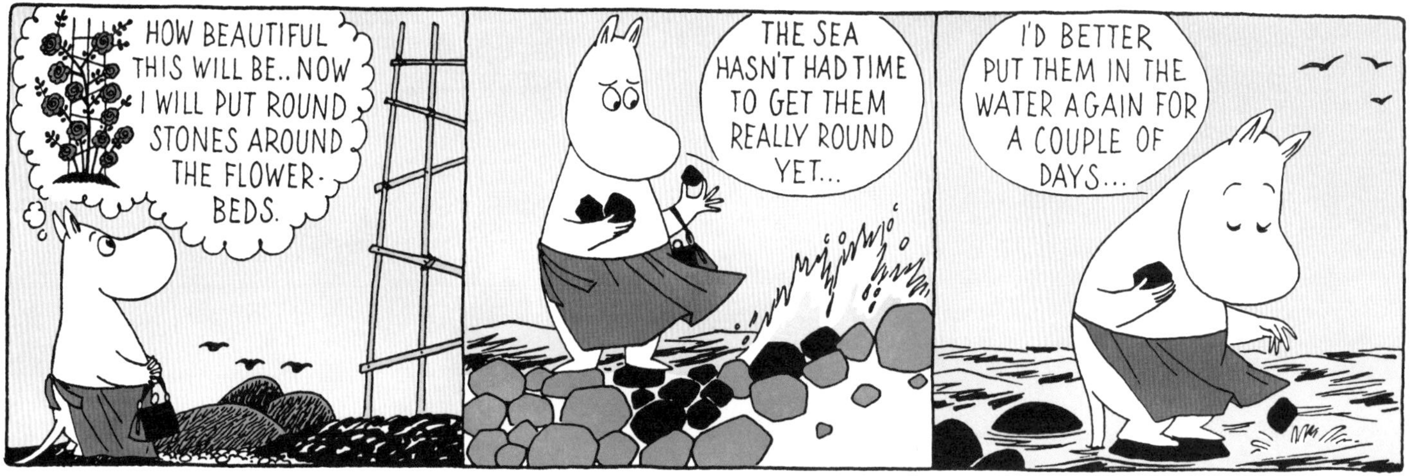
HOW BEAUTIFUL THIS WILL BE.. NOW I WILL PUT ROUND STONES AROUND THE FLOWER-BEDS.
THE SEA HASN'T HAD TIME TO GET THEM REALLY ROUND YET...
I'D BETTER PUT THEM IN THE WATER AGAIN FOR A COUPLE OF DAYS...

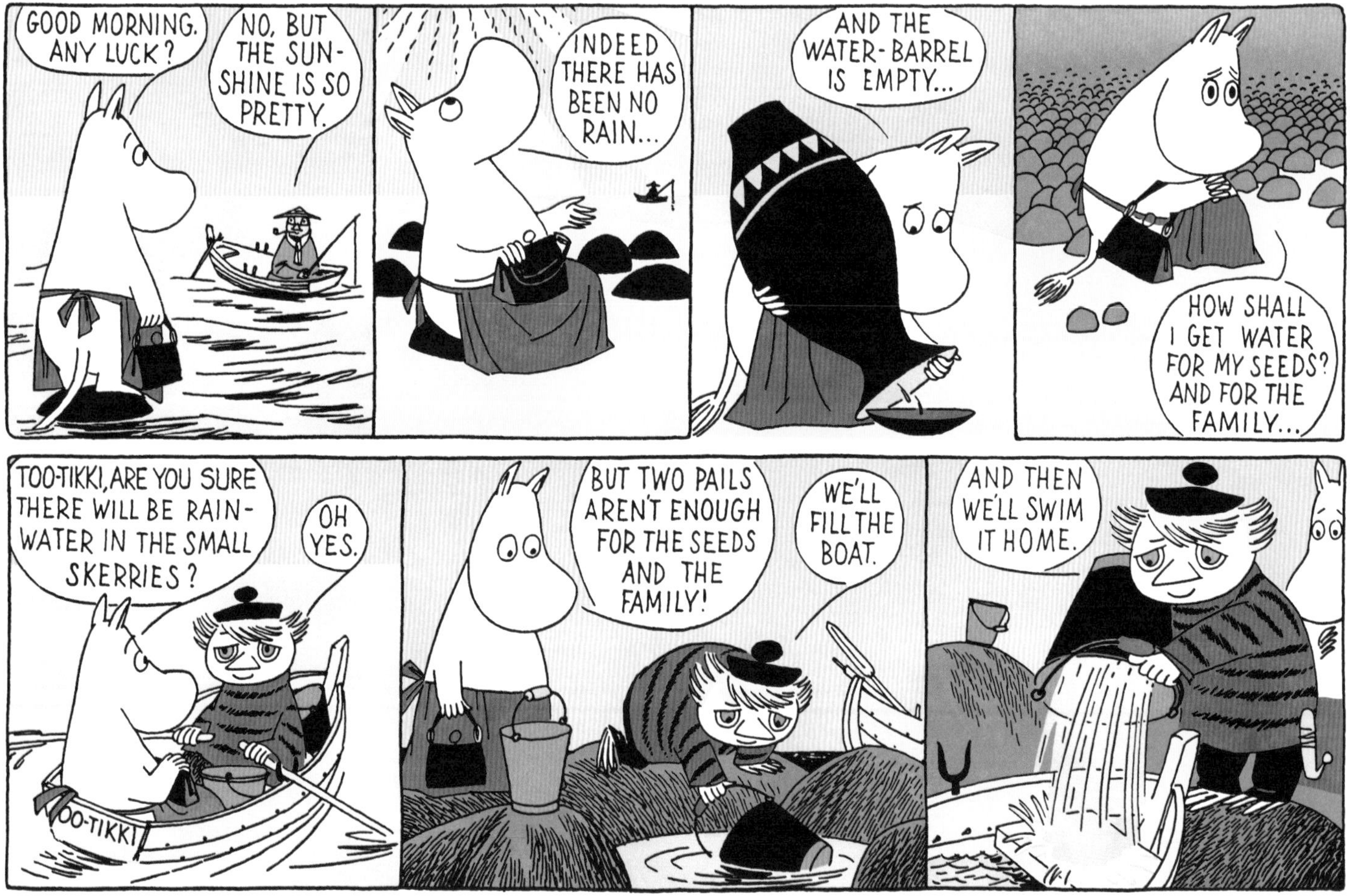
GOOD MORNING. ANY LUCK?
NO, BUT THE SUN-SHINE IS SO PRETTY.
INDEED THERE HAS BEEN NO RAIN...
AND THE WATER-BARREL IS EMPTY...
HOW SHALL I GET WATER FOR MY SEEDS? AND FOR THE FAMILY...
TOO-TIKKI, ARE YOU SURE THERE WILL BE RAIN-WATER IN THE SMALL SKERRIES?
OH YES.
OO-TIKKI
BUT TWO PAILS AREN'T ENOUGH FOR THE SEEDS AND THE FAMILY!
WE'LL FILL THE BOAT.
AND THEN WE'LL SWIM IT HOME.

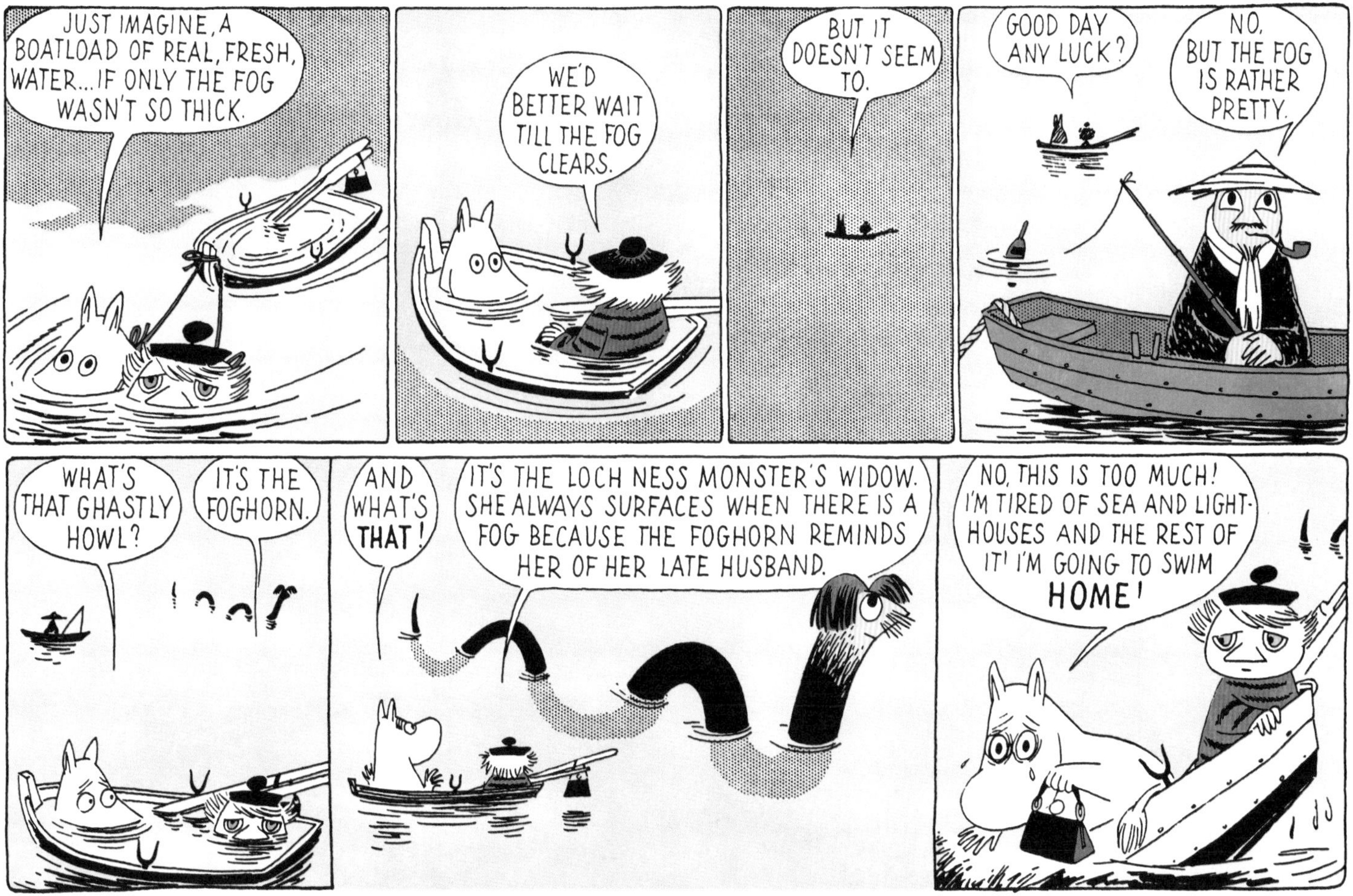
JUST IMAGINE, A BOATLOAD OF REAL, FRESH, WATER... IF ONLY THE FOG WASN'T SO THICK.
WE'D BETTER WAIT TILL THE FOG CLEARS.
BUT IT DOESN'T SEEM TO.
GOOD DAY ANY LUCK?
NO, BUT THE FOG IS RATHER PRETTY.
WHAT'S THAT GHASTLY HOWL?
IT'S THE FOGHORN.
AND WHAT'S **THAT**!
IT'S THE LOCH NESS MONSTER'S WIDOW. SHE ALWAYS SURFACES WHEN THERE IS A FOG BECAUSE THE FOGHORN REMINDS HER OF HER LATE HUSBAND.
NO, THIS IS TOO MUCH! I'M TIRED OF SEA AND LIGHT-HOUSES AND THE REST OF IT! I'M GOING TO SWIM **HOME**!

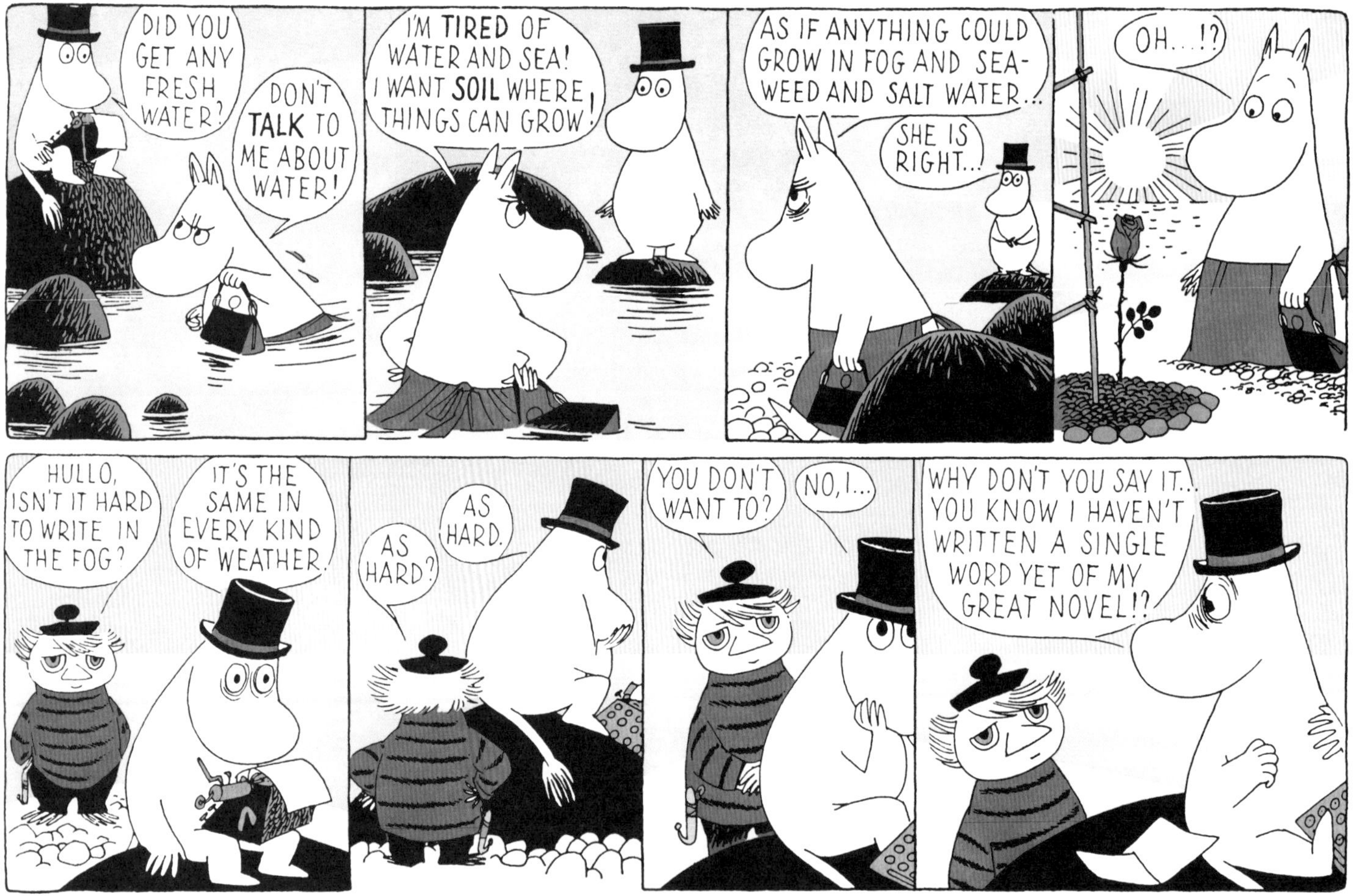
DID YOU GET ANY FRESH WATER?
DON'T TALK TO ME ABOUT WATER!
I'M TIRED OF WATER AND SEA! I WANT SOIL WHERE THINGS CAN GROW!
AS IF ANYTHING COULD GROW IN FOG AND SEA-WEED AND SALT WATER...
SHE IS RIGHT...
OH...!?
HULLO, ISN'T IT HARD TO WRITE IN THE FOG?
IT'S THE SAME IN EVERY KIND OF WEATHER.
AS HARD?
AS HARD.
YOU DON'T WANT TO?
NO, I...
WHY DON'T YOU SAY IT... YOU KNOW I HAVEN'T WRITTEN A SINGLE WORD YET OF MY GREAT NOVEL!?

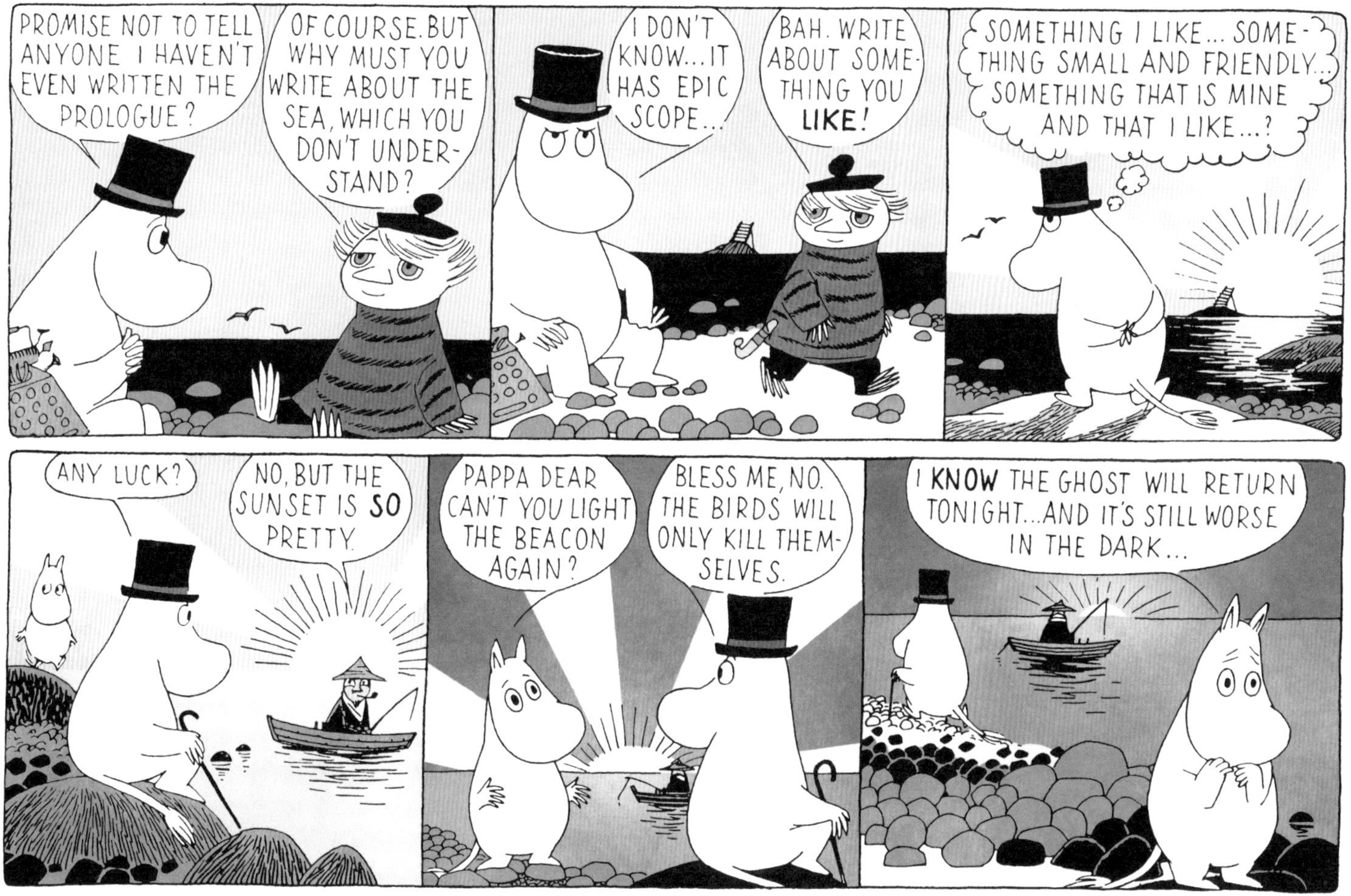
PROMISE NOT TO TELL ANYONE I HAVEN'T EVEN WRITTEN THE PROLOGUE?
OF COURSE. BUT WHY MUST YOU WRITE ABOUT THE SEA, WHICH YOU DON'T UNDERSTAND?
I DON'T KNOW... IT HAS EPIC SCOPE...
BAH. WRITE ABOUT SOMETHING YOU **LIKE**!
SOMETHING I LIKE... SOMETHING SMALL AND FRIENDLY... SOMETHING THAT IS MINE AND THAT I LIKE...?
ANY LUCK?
NO, BUT THE SUNSET IS **SO** PRETTY.
PAPPA DEAR CAN'T YOU LIGHT THE BEACON AGAIN?
BLESS ME, NO. THE BIRDS WILL ONLY KILL THEMSELVES.
I **KNOW** THE GHOST WILL RETURN TONIGHT...AND IT'S STILL WORSE IN THE DARK...

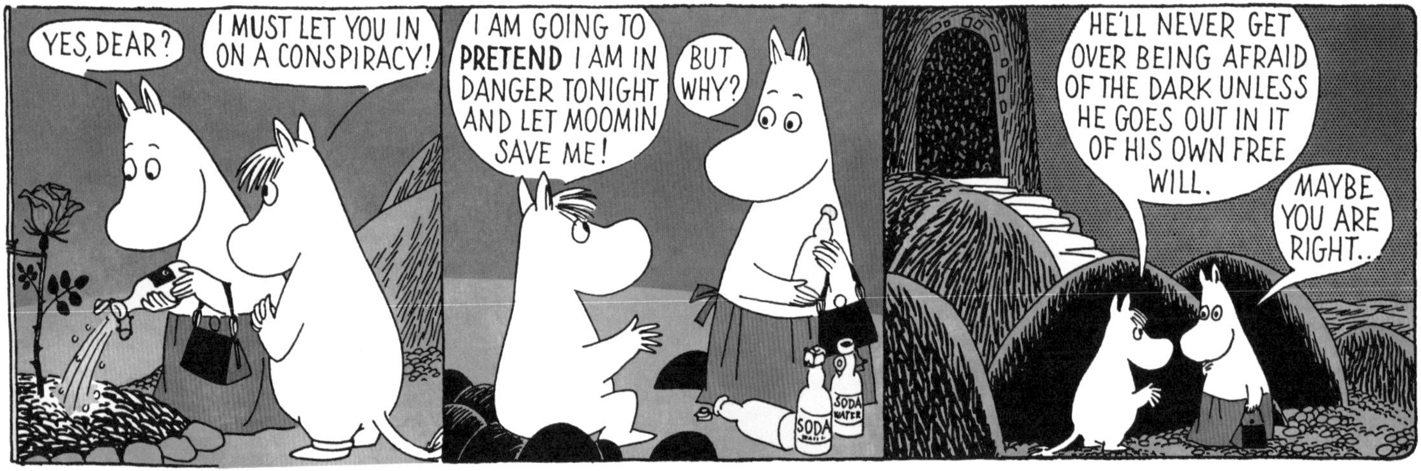
YES, DEAR?
I MUST LET YOU IN ON A CONSPIRACY!
I AM GOING TO **PRETEND** I AM IN DANGER TONIGHT AND LET MOOMIN SAVE ME!
BUT WHY?
HE'LL NEVER GET OVER BEING AFRAID OF THE DARK UNLESS HE GOES OUT IN IT OF HIS OWN FREE WILL.
MAYBE YOU ARE RIGHT..

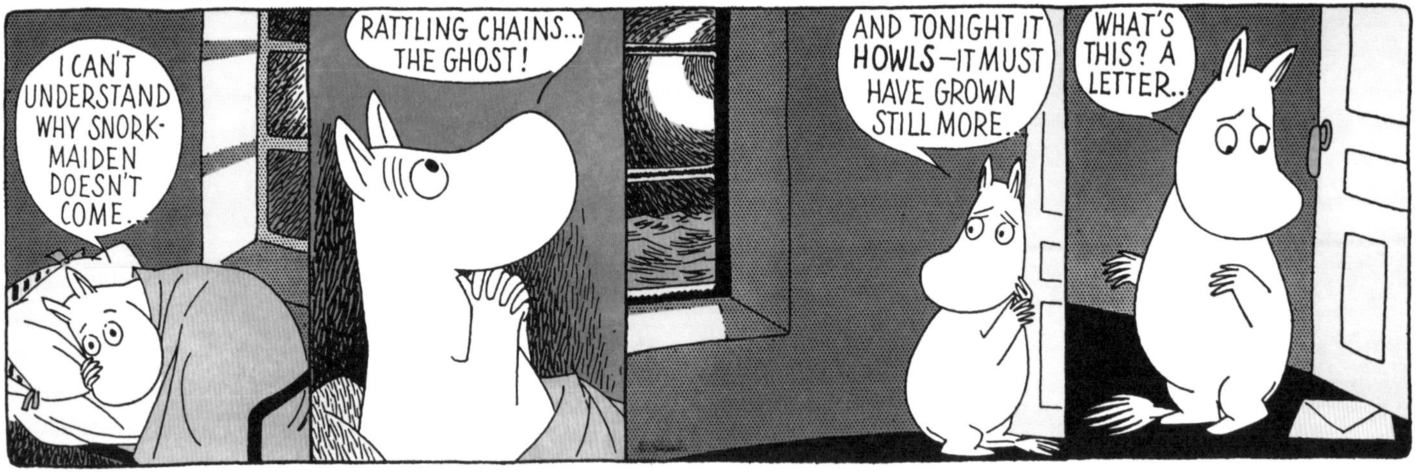
I CAN'T UNDERSTAND WHY SNORK-MAIDEN DOESN'T COME...
RATTLING CHAINS... THE GHOST!
AND TONIGHT IT **HOWLS**—IT MUST HAVE GROWN STILL MORE...
WHAT'S THIS? A LETTER..

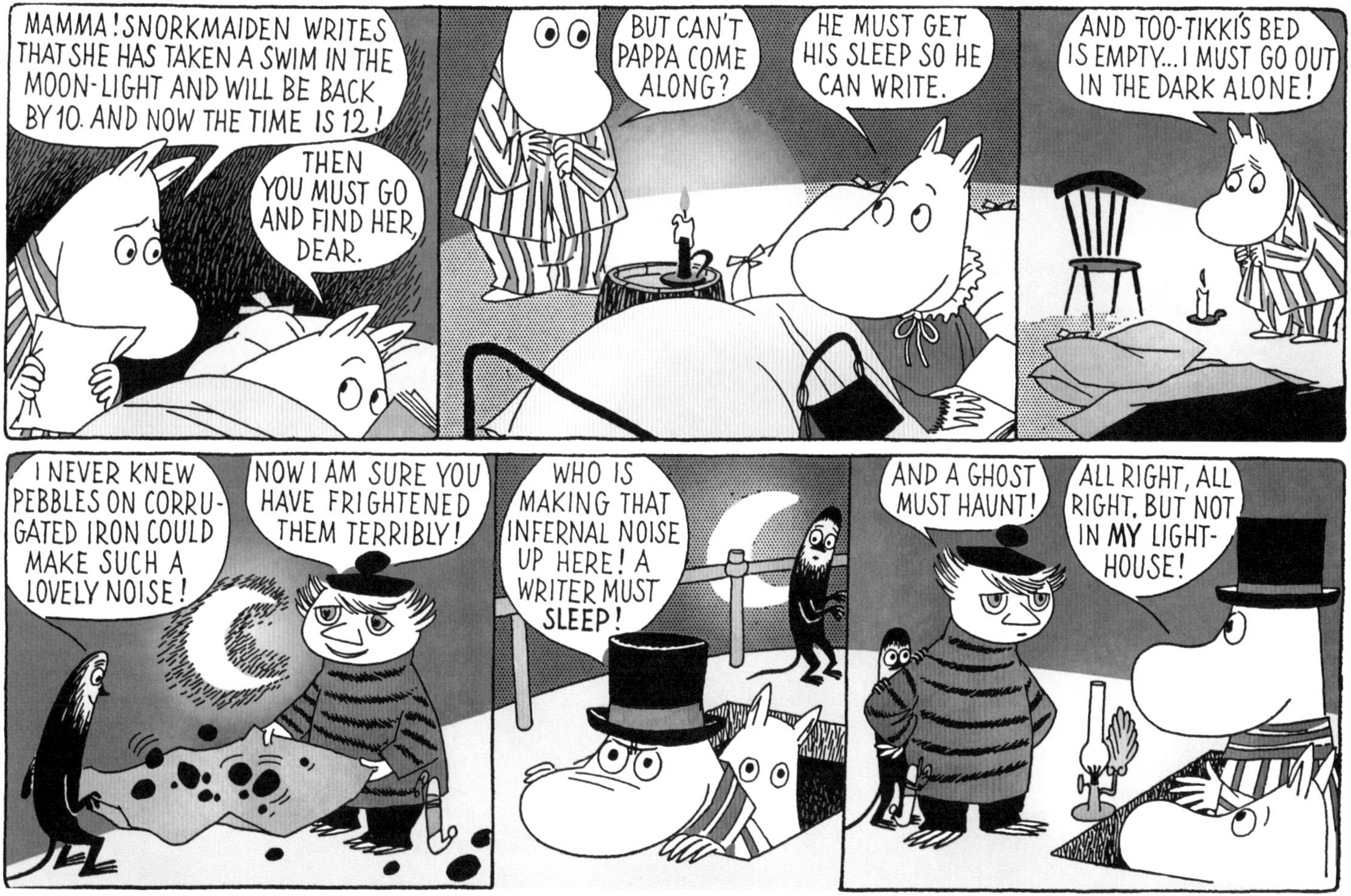
MAMMA! SNORKMAIDEN WRITES THAT SHE HAS TAKEN A SWIM IN THE MOON-LIGHT AND WILL BE BACK BY 10. AND NOW THE TIME IS 12!
THEN YOU MUST GO AND FIND HER, DEAR.
BUT CAN'T PAPPA COME ALONG?
HE MUST GET HIS SLEEP SO HE CAN WRITE.
AND TOO-TIKKI'S BED IS EMPTY... I MUST GO OUT IN THE DARK ALONE!
I NEVER KNEW PEBBLES ON CORRU-GATED IRON COULD MAKE SUCH A LOVELY NOISE!
NOW I AM SURE YOU HAVE FRIGHTENED THEM TERRIBLY!
WHO IS MAKING THAT INFERNAL NOISE UP HERE! A WRITER MUST SLEEP!
AND A GHOST MUST HAUNT!
ALL RIGHT, ALL RIGHT, BUT NOT IN MY LIGHT-HOUSE!

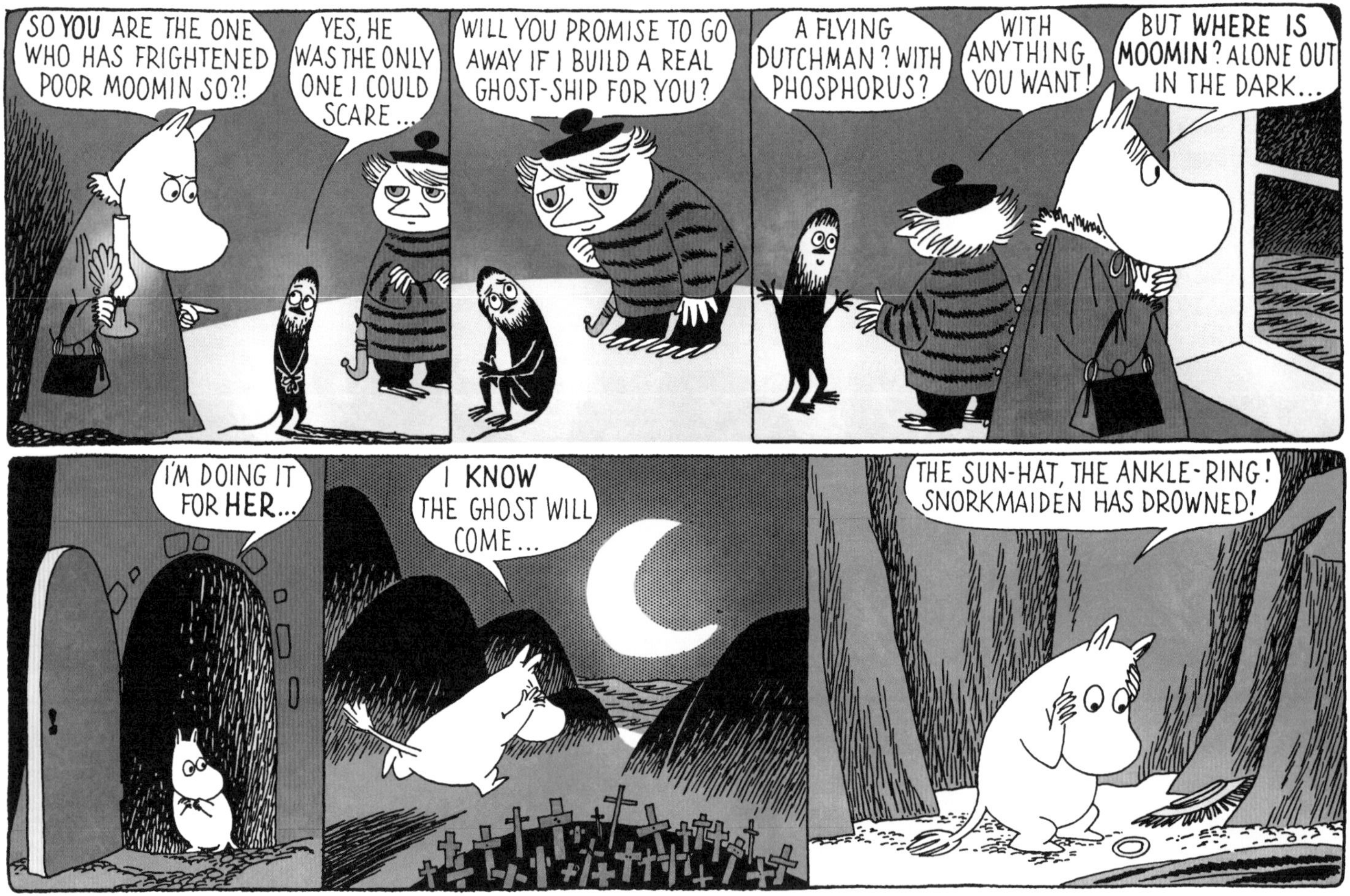
SO YOU ARE THE ONE WHO HAS FRIGHTENED POOR MOOMIN SO?!
YES, HE WAS THE ONLY ONE I COULD SCARE...
WILL YOU PROMISE TO GO AWAY IF I BUILD A REAL GHOST-SHIP FOR YOU?
A FLYING DUTCHMAN? WITH PHOSPHORUS?
WITH ANYTHING YOU WANT!
BUT WHERE IS MOOMIN? ALONE OUT IN THE DARK...
I'M DOING IT FOR HER...
I KNOW THE GHOST WILL COME...
THE SUN-HAT, THE ANKLE-RING! SNORKMAIDEN HAS DROWNED!

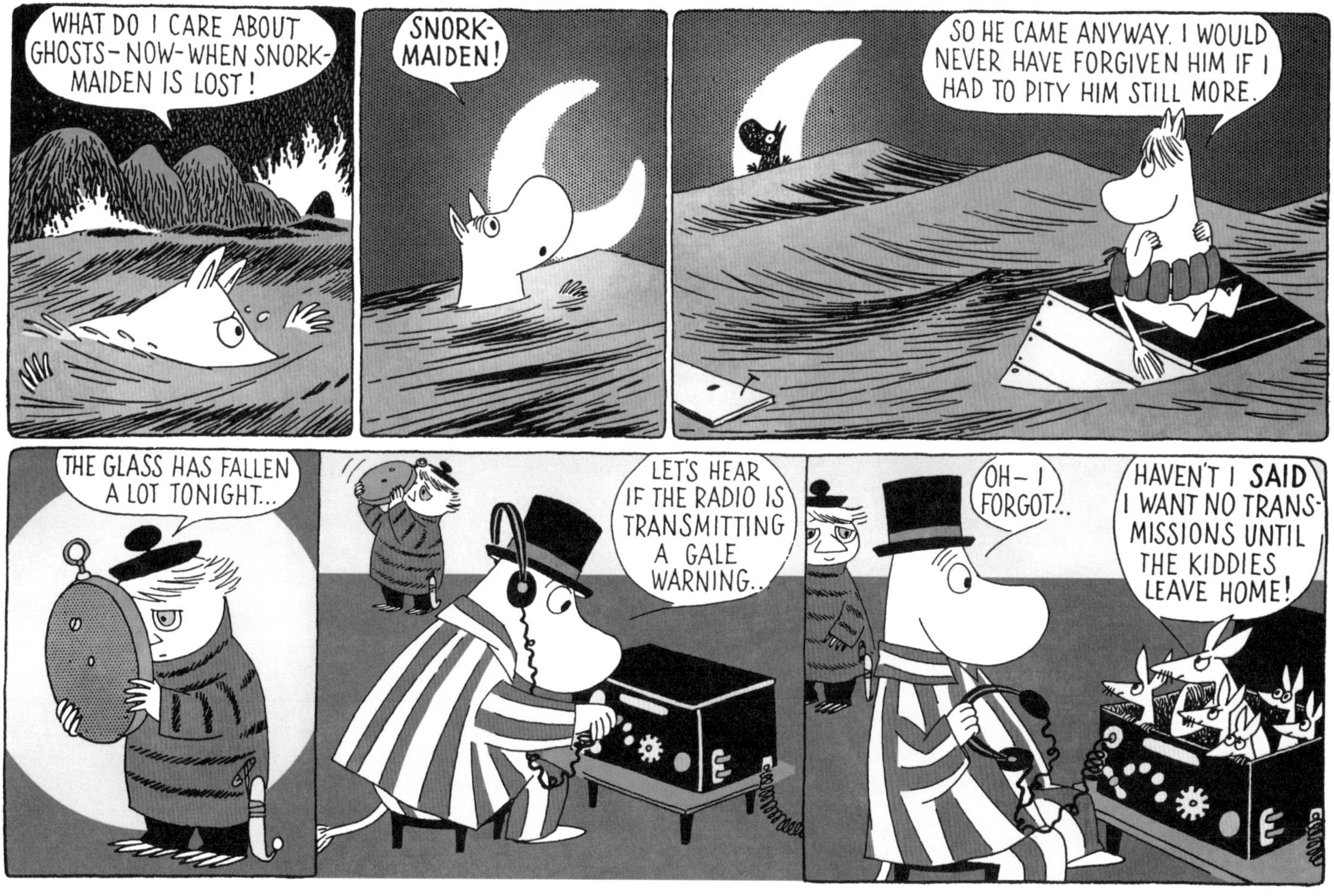
WHAT DO I CARE ABOUT GHOSTS – NOW – WHEN SNORK-MAIDEN IS LOST!
SNORK-MAIDEN!
SO HE CAME ANYWAY. I WOULD NEVER HAVE FORGIVEN HIM IF I HAD TO PITY HIM STILL MORE.
THE GLASS HAS FALLEN A LOT TONIGHT...
LET'S HEAR IF THE RADIO IS TRANSMITTING A GALE WARNING...
OH – I FORGOT...
HAVEN'T I **SAID** I WANT NO TRANSMISSIONS UNTIL THE KIDDIES LEAVE HOME!

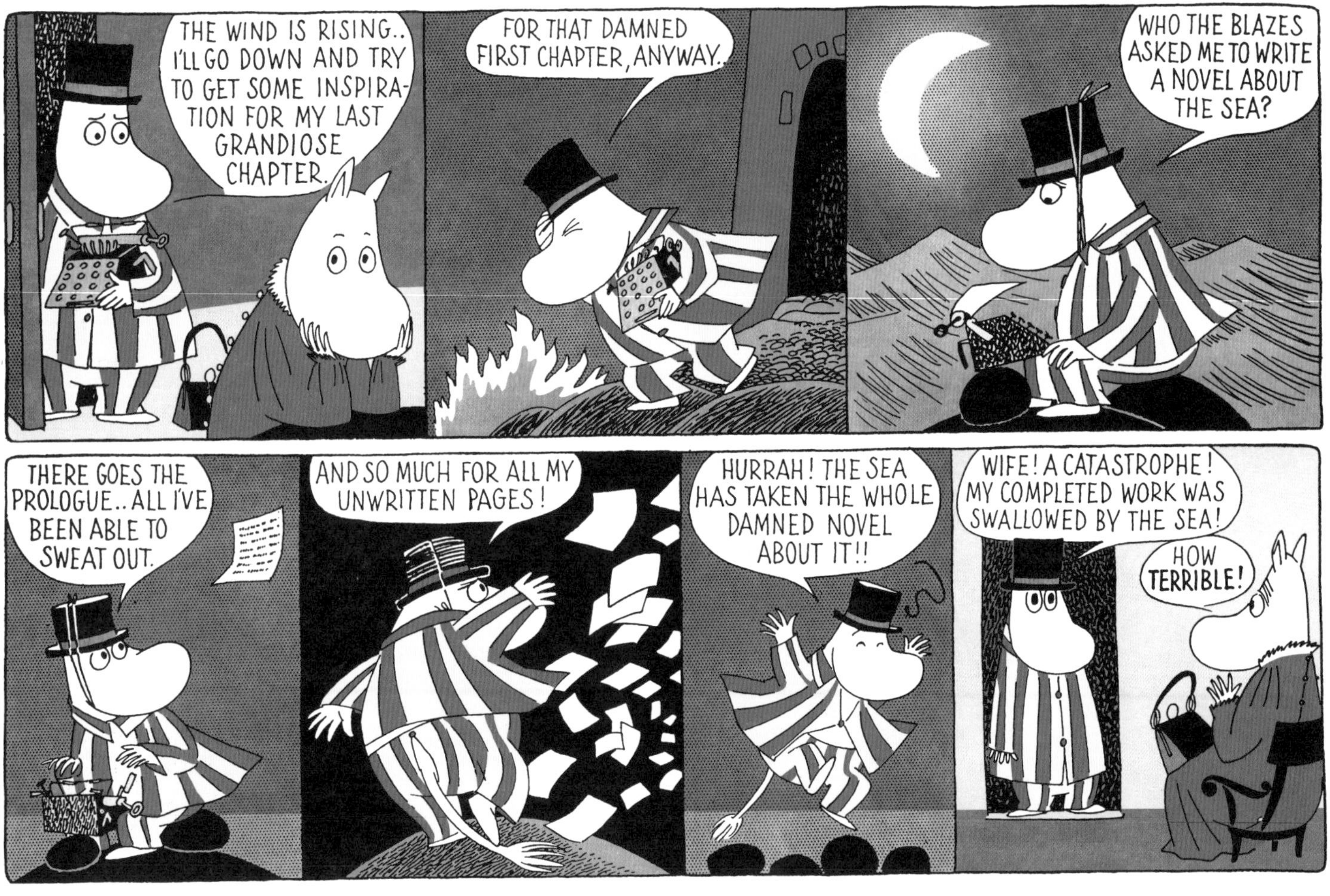
THE WIND IS RISING.. I'LL GO DOWN AND TRY TO GET SOME INSPIRATION FOR MY LAST GRANDIOSE CHAPTER.
FOR THAT DAMNED FIRST CHAPTER, ANYWAY..
WHO THE BLAZES ASKED ME TO WRITE A NOVEL ABOUT THE SEA?
THERE GOES THE PROLOGUE.. ALL I'VE BEEN ABLE TO SWEAT OUT.
AND SO MUCH FOR ALL MY UNWRITTEN PAGES!
HURRAH! THE SEA HAS TAKEN THE WHOLE DAMNED NOVEL ABOUT IT!!
WIFE! A CATASTROPHE! MY COMPLETED WORK WAS SWALLOWED BY THE SEA!
HOW TERRIBLE!

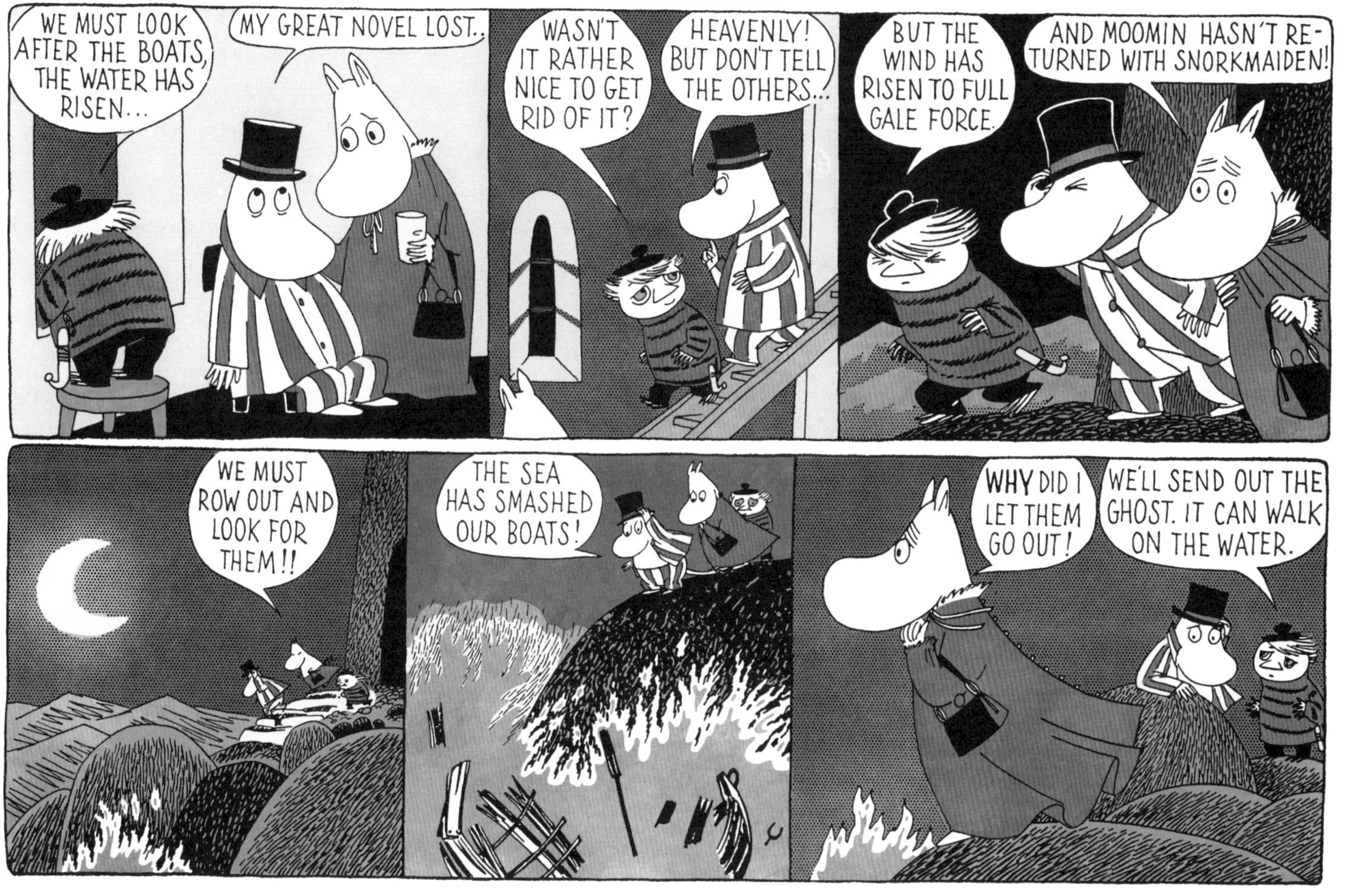
WE MUST LOOK AFTER THE BOATS, THE WATER HAS RISEN...
MY GREAT NOVEL LOST..
WASN'T IT RATHER NICE TO GET RID OF IT?
HEAVENLY! BUT DON'T TELL THE OTHERS...
BUT THE WIND HAS RISEN TO FULL GALE FORCE.
AND MOOMIN HASN'T RETURNED WITH SNORKMAIDEN!
WE MUST ROW OUT AND LOOK FOR THEM!!
THE SEA HAS SMASHED OUR BOATS!
WHY DID I LET THEM GO OUT!
WE'LL SEND OUT THE GHOST. IT CAN WALK ON THE WATER.

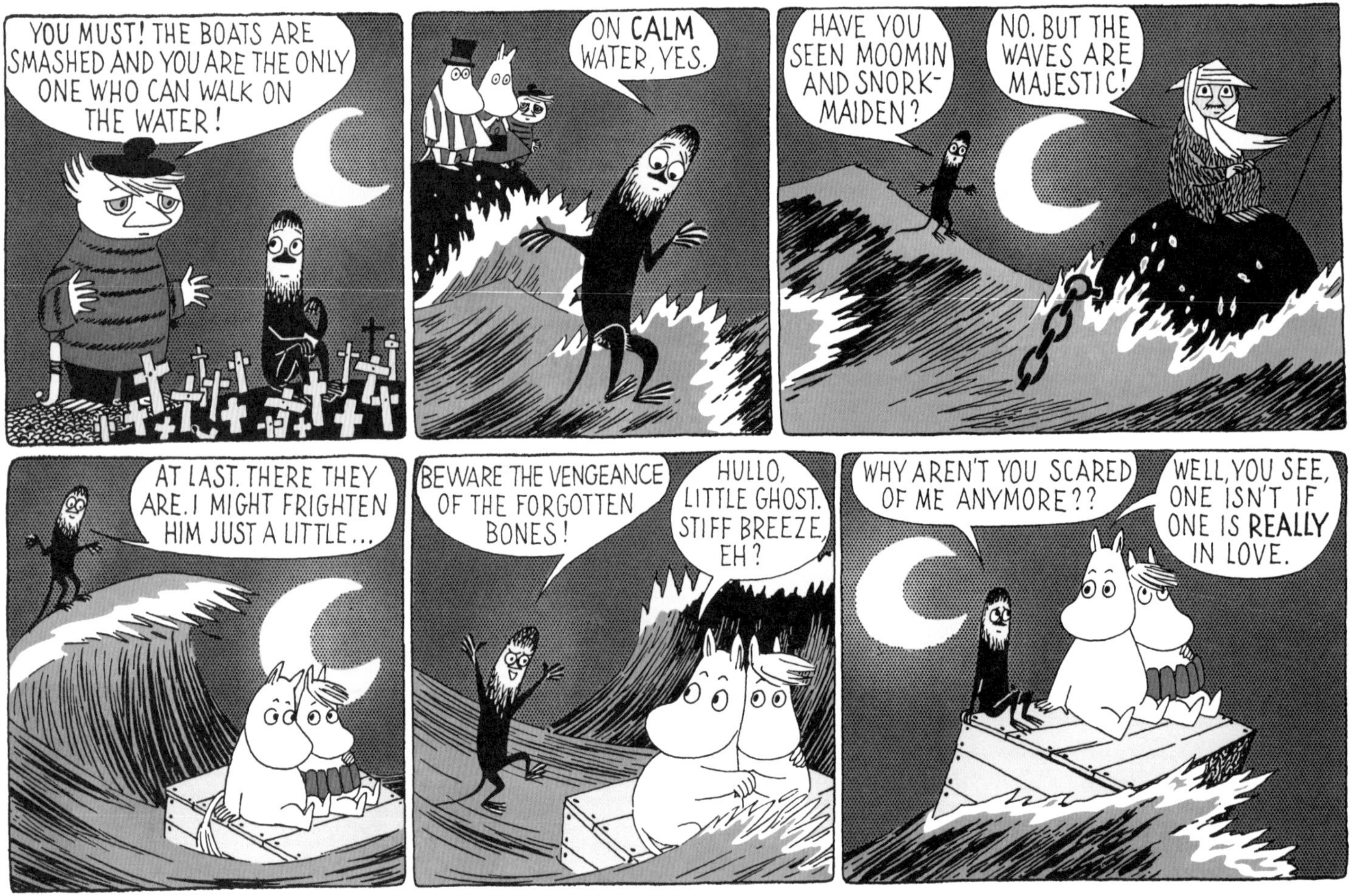
YOU MUST! THE BOATS ARE SMASHED AND YOU ARE THE ONLY ONE WHO CAN WALK ON THE WATER!
ON CALM WATER, YES.
HAVE YOU SEEN MOOMIN AND SNORK-MAIDEN?
NO. BUT THE WAVES ARE MAJESTIC!
AT LAST. THERE THEY ARE. I MIGHT FRIGHTEN HIM JUST A LITTLE...
BEWARE THE VENGEANCE OF THE FORGOTTEN BONES!
HULLO, LITTLE GHOST. STIFF BREEZE, EH?
WHY AREN'T YOU SCARED OF ME ANYMORE??
WELL, YOU SEE, ONE ISN'T IF ONE IS REALLY IN LOVE.

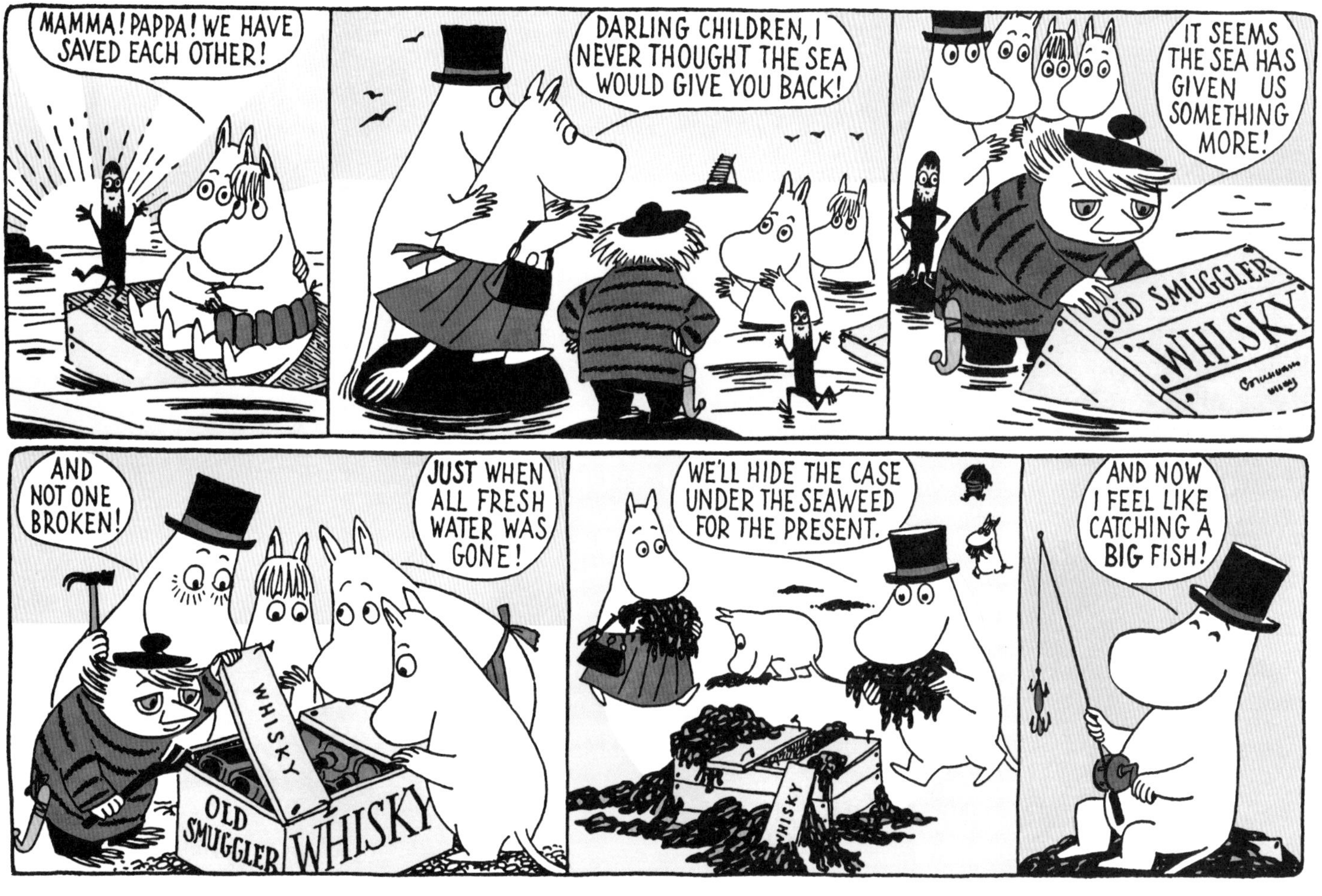
MAMMA! PAPPA! WE HAVE SAVED EACH OTHER!
DARLING CHILDREN, I NEVER THOUGHT THE SEA WOULD GIVE YOU BACK!
IT SEEMS THE SEA HAS GIVEN US SOMETHING MORE!
OLD SMUGGLER WHISKY
AND NOT ONE BROKEN!
JUST WHEN ALL FRESH WATER WAS GONE!
WHISKY
OLD SMUGGLER WHISKY
WE'LL HIDE THE CASE UNDER THE SEAWEED FOR THE PRESENT.
WHISKY
AND NOW I FEEL LIKE CATCHING A BIG FISH!

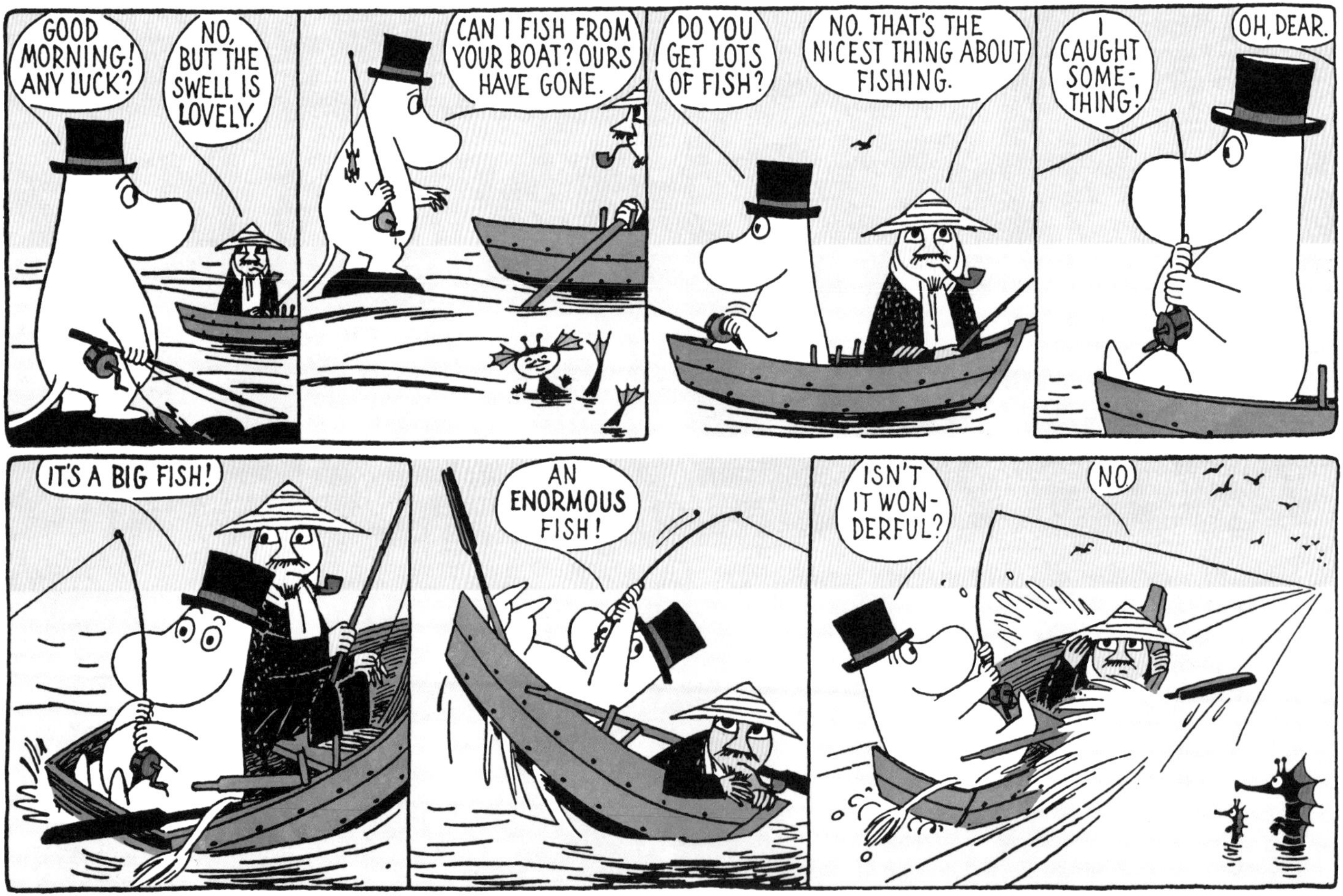

GOOD MORNING! ANY LUCK?
NO, BUT THE SWELL IS LOVELY.
CAN I FISH FROM YOUR BOAT? OURS HAVE GONE.
DO YOU GET LOTS OF FISH?
NO. THAT'S THE NICEST THING ABOUT FISHING.
I CAUGHT SOME-THING!
OH, DEAR.
IT'S A BIG FISH!
AN ENORMOUS FISH!
ISN'T IT WON-DERFUL?
NO

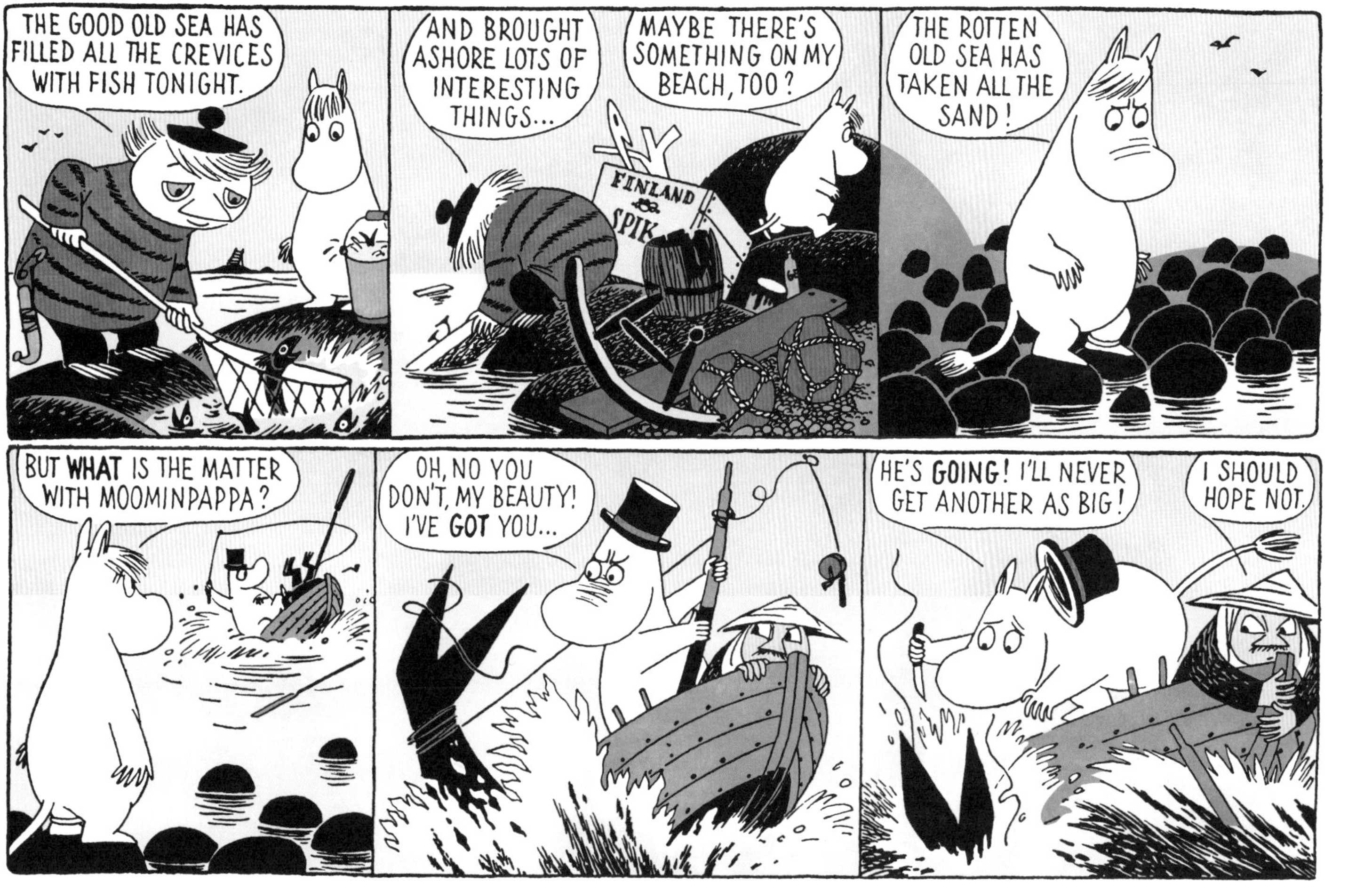
THE GOOD OLD SEA HAS FILLED ALL THE CREVICES WITH FISH TONIGHT.
AND BROUGHT ASHORE LOTS OF INTERESTING THINGS...
MAYBE THERE'S SOMETHING ON MY BEACH, TOO?
FINLAND
SPIK
THE ROTTEN OLD SEA HAS TAKEN ALL THE SAND!
BUT **WHAT** IS THE MATTER WITH MOOMINPAPPA?
OH, NO YOU DON'T, MY BEAUTY! I'VE **GOT** YOU...
HE'S **GOING**! I'LL NEVER GET ANOTHER AS BIG!
I SHOULD HOPE NOT.

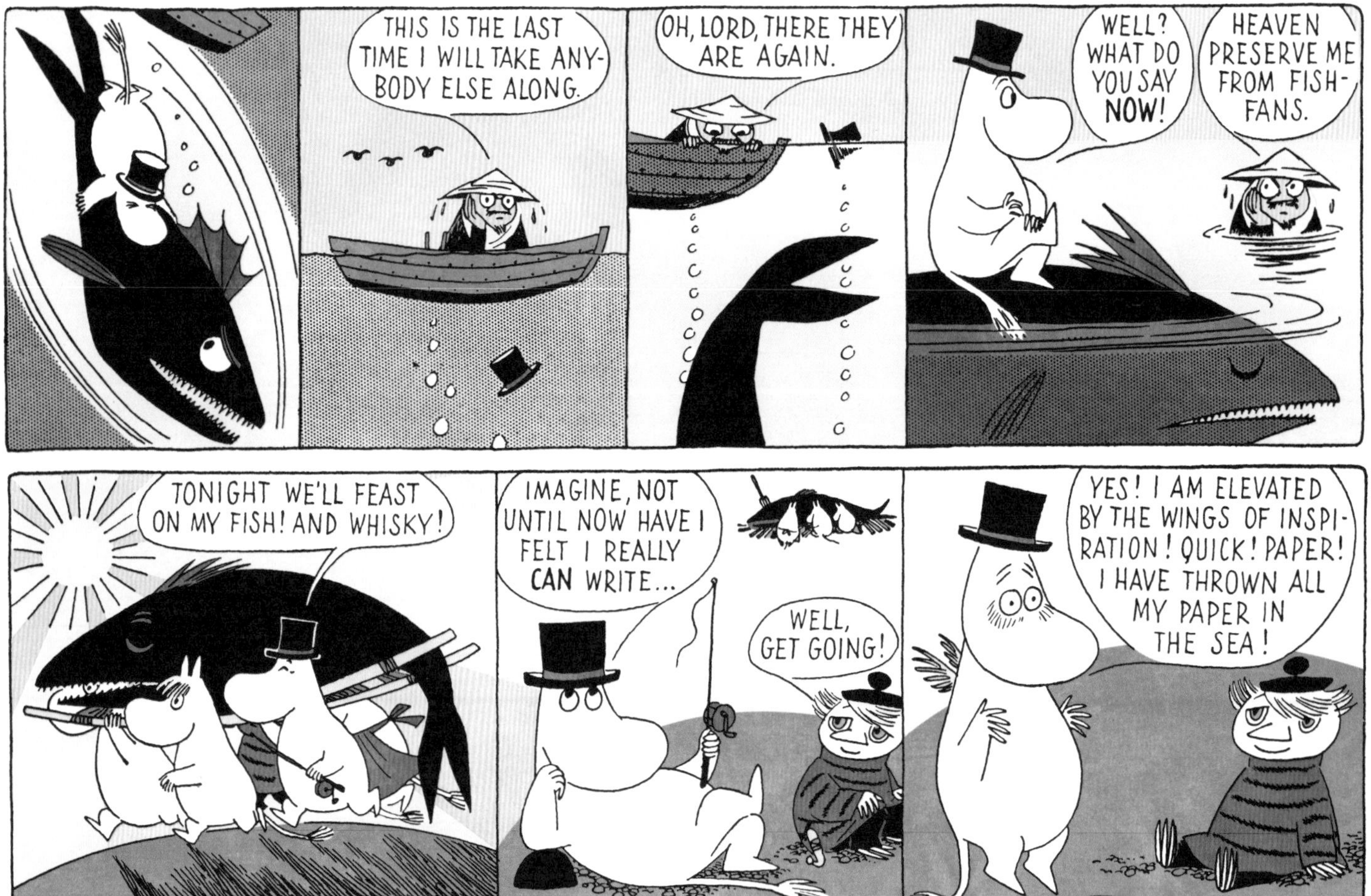
THIS IS THE LAST TIME I WILL TAKE ANY-BODY ELSE ALONG.
OH, LORD, THERE THEY ARE AGAIN.
WELL? WHAT DO YOU SAY **NOW**!
HEAVEN PRESERVE ME FROM FISH-FANS.
TONIGHT WE'LL FEAST ON MY FISH! AND WHISKY!
IMAGINE, NOT UNTIL NOW HAVE I FELT I REALLY **CAN** WRITE...
WELL, GET GOING!
YES! I AM ELEVATED BY THE WINGS OF INSPI-RATION! QUICK! PAPER! I HAVE THROWN ALL MY PAPER IN THE SEA!

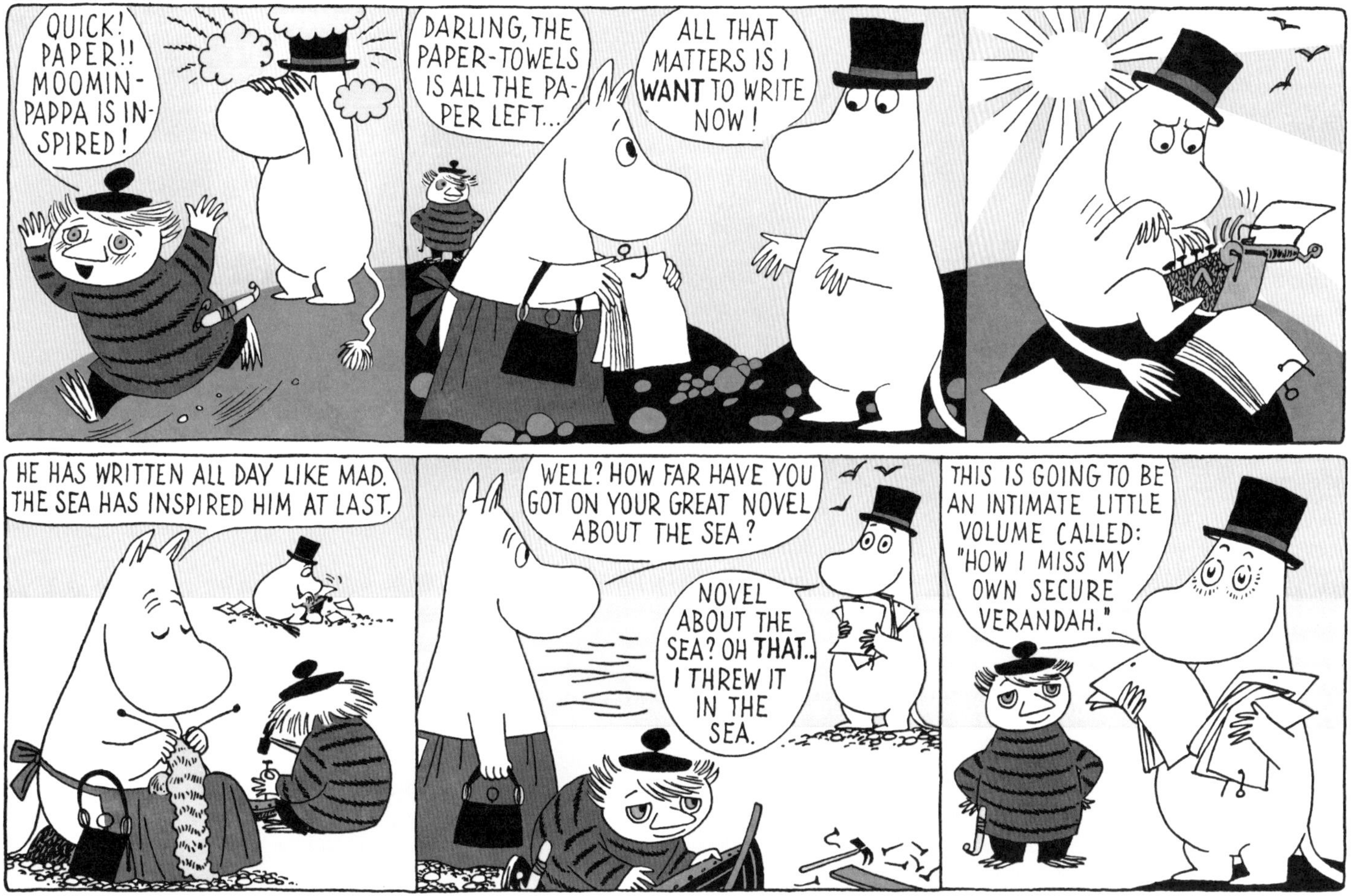
QUICK! PAPER!! MOOMIN-PAPPA IS IN-SPIRED!
DARLING, THE PAPER-TOWELS IS ALL THE PA-PER LEFT...
ALL THAT MATTERS IS I **WANT** TO WRITE NOW!
HE HAS WRITTEN ALL DAY LIKE MAD. THE SEA HAS INSPIRED HIM AT LAST.
WELL? HOW FAR HAVE YOU GOT ON YOUR GREAT NOVEL ABOUT THE SEA?
NOVEL ABOUT THE SEA? OH **THAT**.. I THREW IT IN THE SEA.
THIS IS GOING TO BE AN INTIMATE LITTLE VOLUME CALLED: "HOW I MISS MY OWN SECURE VERANDAH."

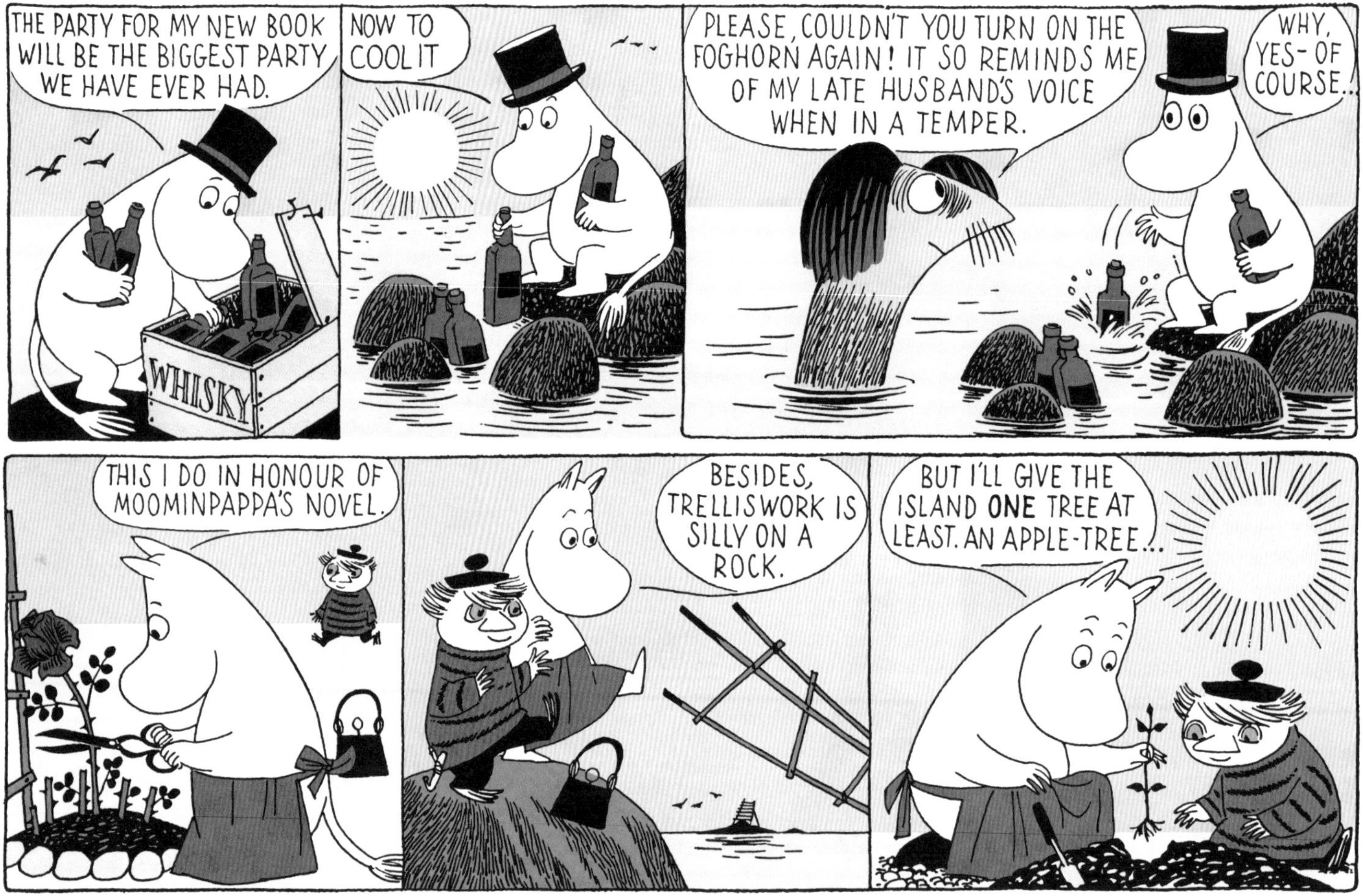
THE PARTY FOR MY NEW BOOK WILL BE THE BIGGEST PARTY WE HAVE EVER HAD.
WHISKY
NOW TO COOL IT
PLEASE, COULDN'T YOU TURN ON THE FOGHORN AGAIN! IT SO REMINDS ME OF MY LATE HUSBAND'S VOICE WHEN IN A TEMPER.
WHY, YES- OF COURSE...
THIS I DO IN HONOUR OF MOOMINPAPPA'S NOVEL.
BESIDES, TRELLISWORK IS SILLY ON A ROCK.
BUT I'LL GIVE THE ISLAND **ONE** TREE AT LEAST. AN APPLE-TREE...

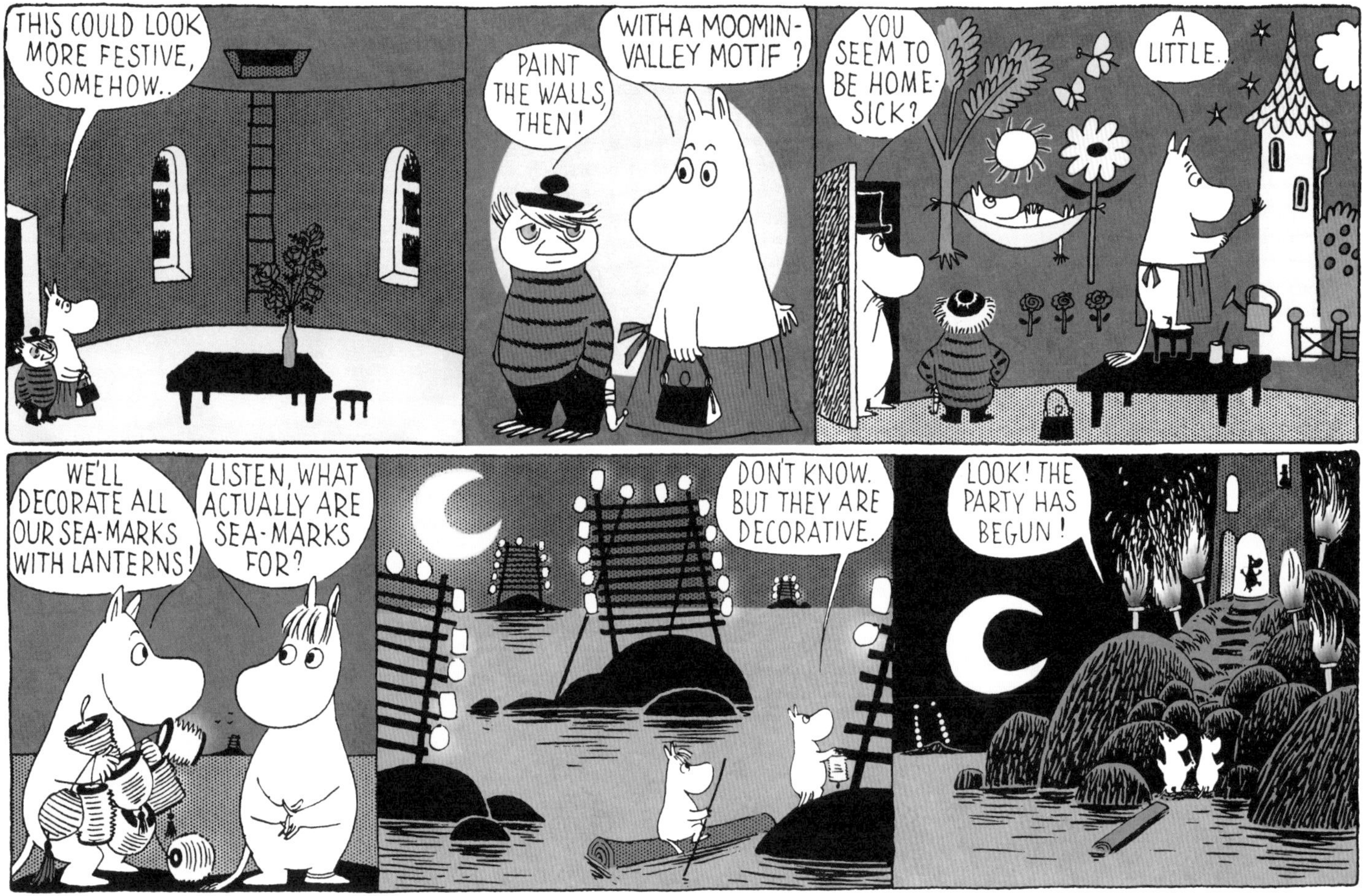
THIS COULD LOOK MORE FESTIVE, SOMEHOW..
PAINT THE WALLS, THEN!
WITH A MOOMIN-VALLEY MOTIF ?
YOU SEEM TO BE HOME-SICK?
A LITTLE..
WE'LL DECORATE ALL OUR SEA-MARKS WITH LANTERNS!
LISTEN, WHAT ACTUALLY ARE SEA-MARKS FOR?
DON'T KNOW. BUT THEY ARE DECORATIVE.
LOOK! THE PARTY HAS BEGUN!

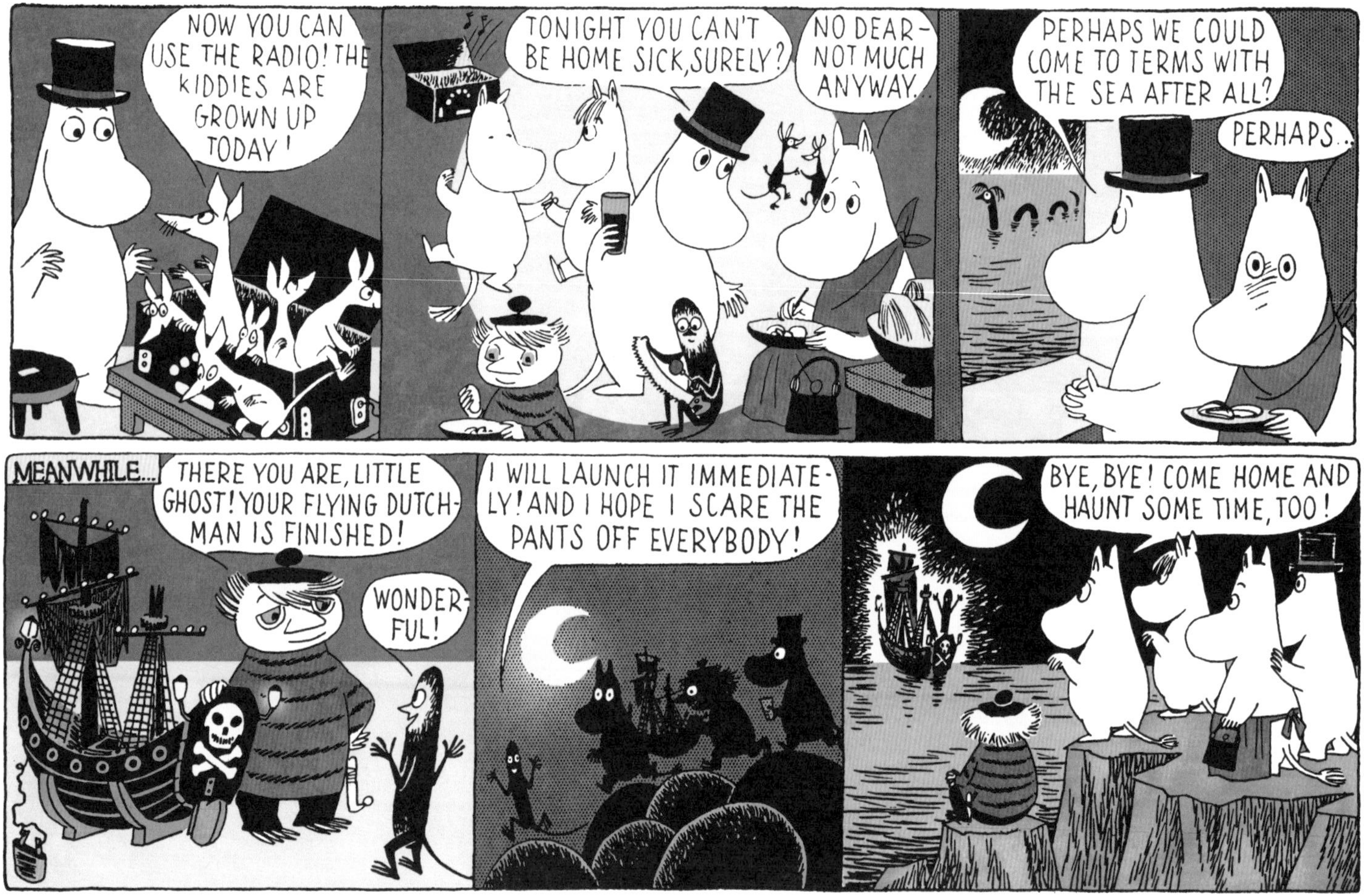
NOW YOU CAN USE THE RADIO! THE KIDDIES ARE GROWN UP TODAY!
TONIGHT YOU CAN'T BE HOME SICK, SURELY?
NO DEAR- NOT MUCH ANYWAY...
PERHAPS WE COULD COME TO TERMS WITH THE SEA AFTER ALL?
PERHAPS...
MEANWHILE...
THERE YOU ARE, LITTLE GHOST! YOUR FLYING DUTCHMAN IS FINISHED!
WONDERFUL!
I WILL LAUNCH IT IMMEDIATELY! AND I HOPE I SCARE THE PANTS OFF EVERYBODY!
BYE, BYE! COME HOME AND HAUNT SOME TIME, TOO!

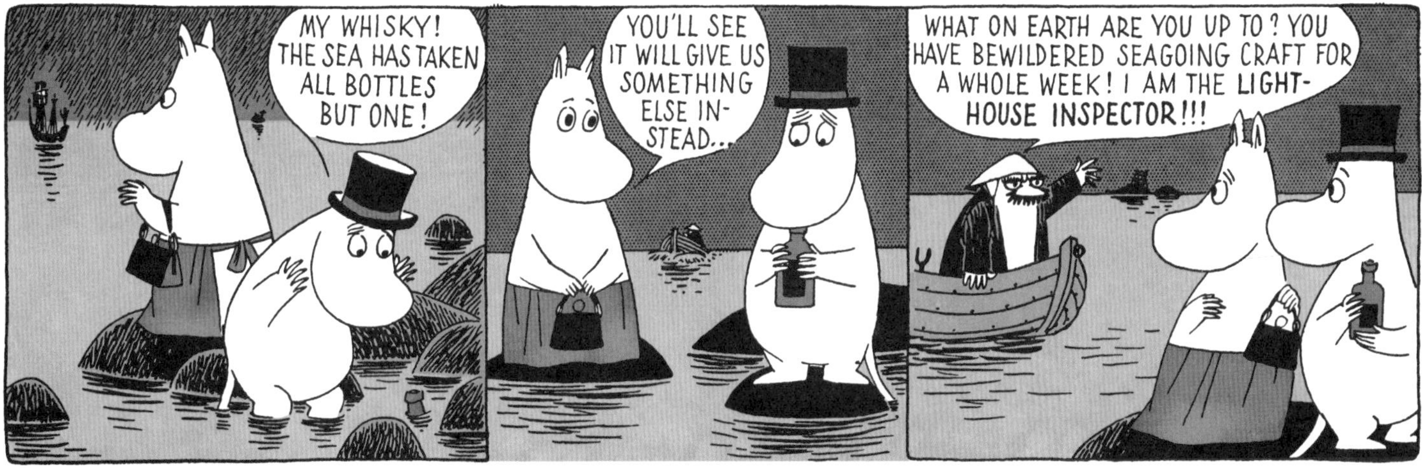
MY WHISKY! THE SEA HAS TAKEN ALL BOTTLES BUT ONE!
YOU'LL SEE IT WILL GIVE US SOMETHING ELSE INSTEAD...
WHAT ON EARTH ARE YOU UP TO? YOU HAVE BEWILDERED SEAGOING CRAFT FOR A WHOLE WEEK! I AM THE LIGHTHOUSE INSPECTOR!!!
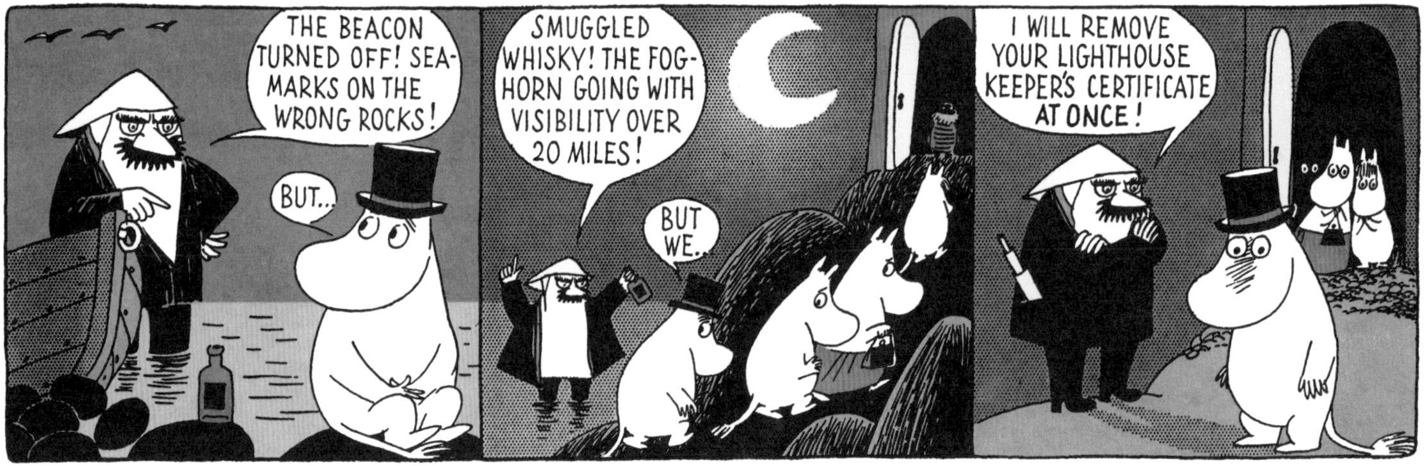
THE BEACON TURNED OFF! SEAMARKS ON THE WRONG ROCKS!
BUT...
SMUGGLED WHISKY! THE FOGHORN GOING WITH VISIBILITY OVER 20 MILES!
BUT WE...
I WILL REMOVE YOUR LIGHTHOUSE KEEPER'S CERTIFICATE AT ONCE!

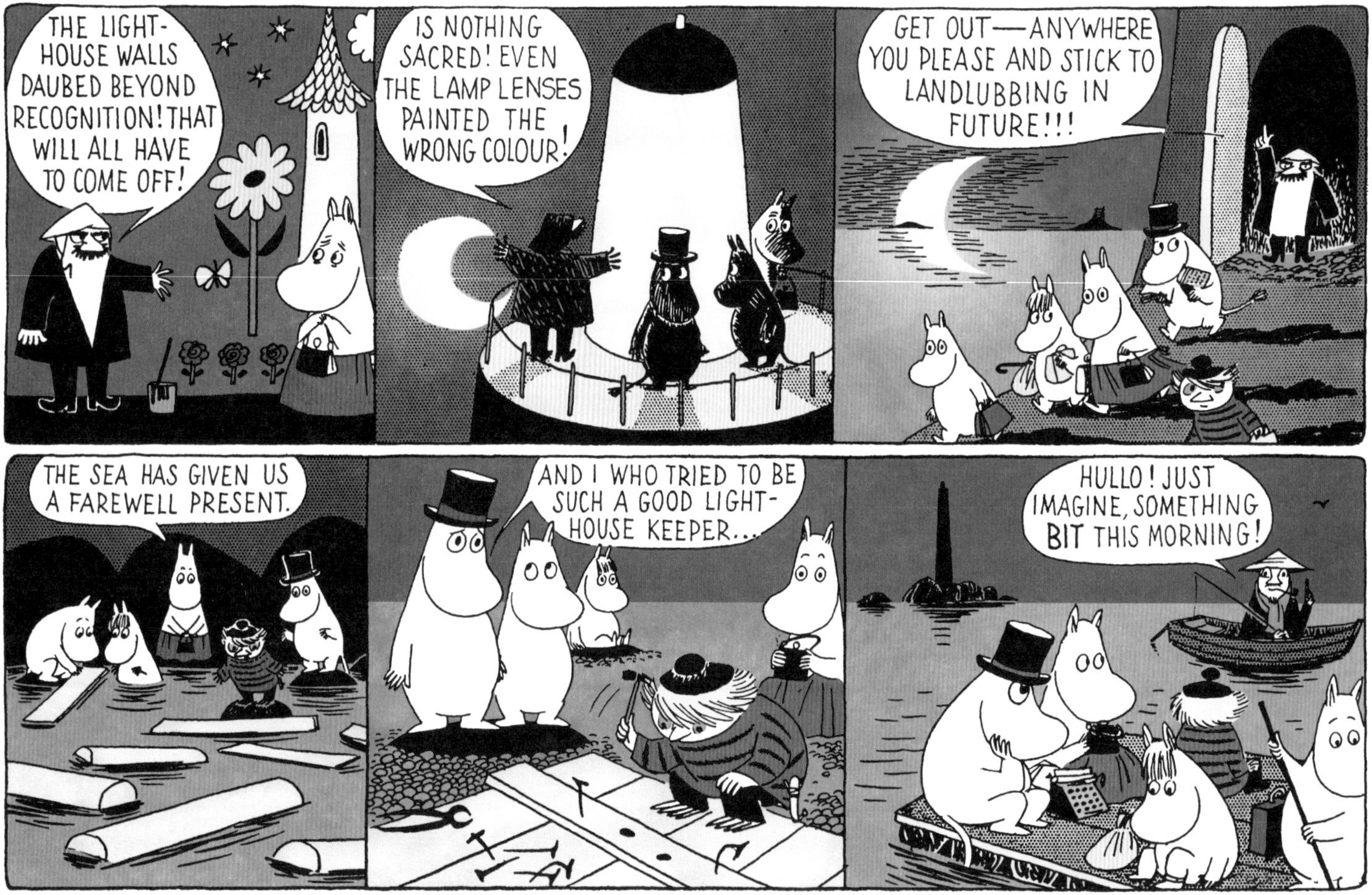
THE LIGHT-HOUSE WALLS DAUBED BEYOND RECOGNITION! THAT WILL ALL HAVE TO COME OFF!
IS NOTHING SACRED! EVEN THE LAMP LENSES PAINTED THE WRONG COLOUR!
GET OUT—ANYWHERE YOU PLEASE AND STICK TO LANDLUBBING IN FUTURE!!!
THE SEA HAS GIVEN US A FAREWELL PRESENT.
AND I WHO TRIED TO BE SUCH A GOOD LIGHT-HOUSE KEEPER...
HULLO! JUST IMAGINE, SOMETHING BIT THIS MORNING!

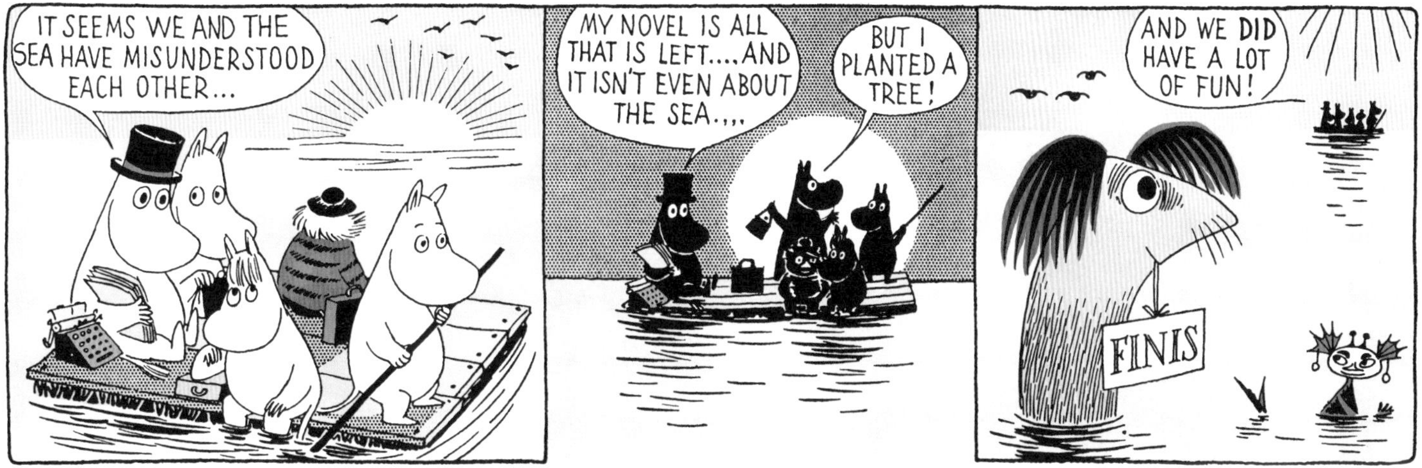
IT SEEMS WE AND THE SEA HAVE MISUNDERSTOOD EACH OTHER...
MY NOVEL IS ALL THAT IS LEFT....AND IT ISN'T EVEN ABOUT THE SEA...,
BUT I PLANTED A TREE!
AND WE **DID** HAVE A LOT OF FUN!
FINIS

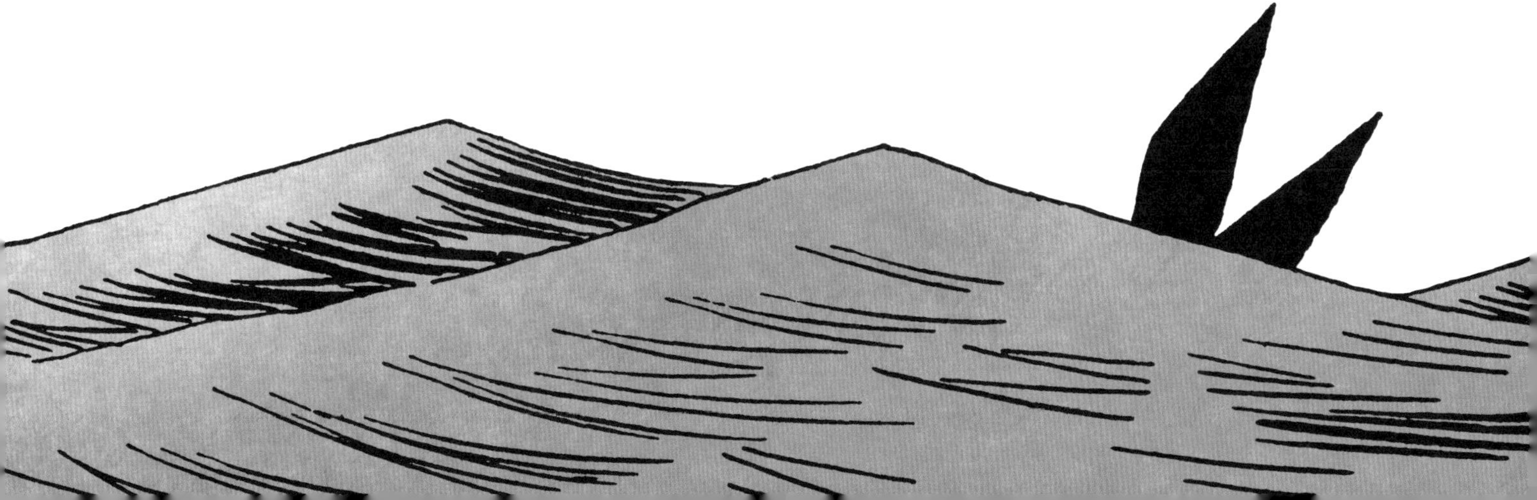

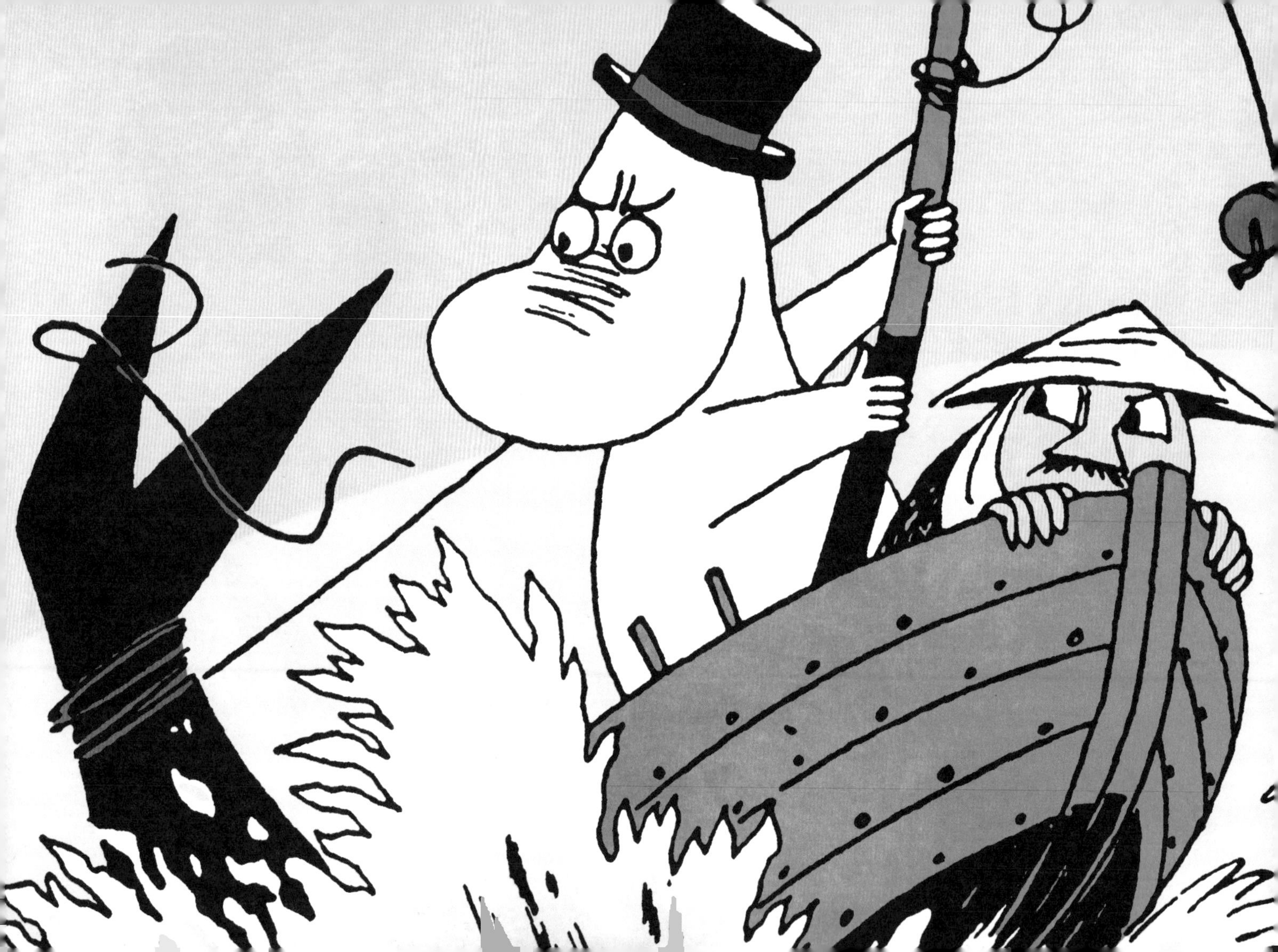